JOUSTING WITH GIANTS

JOUSTING WITH GIANTS

THE JIM McLEAN STORY

Jim McLean
WITH KEN GALLACHER

MAINSTREAM PUBLISHING

Copyright © Jim McLean and Ken Gallacher, 1987
All rights reserved

First published in 1987 by
MAINSTREAM PUBLISHING COMPANY
(EDINBURGH) LTD.
7 Albany Street
Edinburgh EH1 3UG

ISBN 1 85158 088 3 (cloth)

No part of this book may be reproduced or transmitted in any form or by any means, mechanical or electric, including photocopy, recording or any information storage and retrieval system now known or to be invented, without permission in writing from the publisher, except by a reviewer who wishes to quote brief passages in connection with a review for insertion in a magazine, newspaper or broadcast.

British Library Cataloguing in Publication Data

McLean, Jim
   Jousting with giants : the Jim McLean story.
   1. McLean, Jim 2. Soccer managers—
   Scotland——Biography
   I. Title II. Gallacher, Ken
   796.334'092'4   GV942.7.M27/

ISBN 1-85158-088-3

Typeset by Pulse Origination, Edinburgh.
Printed by Billing & Sons, Worcester.

*To my mother and father
for all they have done for me.*

Contents

1	*A VISIT CHANGES MY LIFE*	11
2	*RANGERS AND THE OFFER I COULD REFUSE*	26
3	*BRUTALITY IN THE PREMIER LEAGUE*	37
4	*TOPPLING THE GIANTS*	50
5	*SO CLOSE TO GLORY IN GOTHENBURG*	70
6	*POPULARITY IS OUT*	89
7	*A HANGER-ON WITH SCOTLAND*	101
8	*AN AFTERNOON OF FEAR IN ROME*	112
9	*MY LOVE AFFAIR WITH DUNDEE UNITED*	127
10	*TROPHY WINS AND HAMPDEN HEARTBREAKS*	142
11	*THE PLAYERS WHO MADE IT POSSIBLE*	157

Acknowledgement

The people I want to thank most of all are John Prentice and the directors of Dundee United, in particular Johnstone Grant and George Fox; the various members of my backroom staff over the years, Andy Dickson, Ian Campbell, Graeme Lowe, Walter Smith, Gordon Wallace and all of the Scouts. Most of all I have to thank the players — every player who has ever played for me, whether they have been successful or not. Any success I have had would not have been possible without them.

Chapter One

A VISIT CHANGES MY LIFE

All the way through my career as a player I was dogged by an inferiority complex and it's something which has worried me during my time as a manager too. It has always been a major problem that I have lacked confidence in myself — and, often enough, lacked confidence in my teams. Maybe that has changed a little over the past few years but it remains a nagging worry.

Probably because of that inferiority complex I had never thought about staying on in the game when my playing career came to an end. Nor did I think that anyone would seriously offer me a job as a coach or a manager. I had always had fairly strong views on how the game should be played but as far as I was concerned when my playing days ended I was going to go back to my trade as a joiner. What happened to me can be summed up in one man's name — John Prentice!

He came to see me at my house in Dundee one night just as I was nearing the end of my time as a player. I had been at Dens Park for a few seasons and then left there to go to Kilmarnock. It was the close season when he arrived to see me and his offer came out of the blue. It still seems incredible to me that John Prentice would want me as a coach. He must have been able to see something in me which I couldn't see myself. No one else would have offered me that job. I'm convinced of that.

That close season I was planning on building another house. It was the way I spent the close seasons back then. I had started off building a semi-detached with my brother Willie in our home village of Ashgill. Then, following that, I built a house in Dundee and unhappily that affected my performances when I was a player at Dens Park. It was just during the last little bit of my spell there and I think the way I played in that time encouraged them to sell me to Kilmarnock. I was always sure that I would be going back to the tools, so that as far as I was concerned building houses kept my hand in for the time when playing football stopped.

Then came that visit from John Prentice. It's no exaggeration to say that it changed my life. Everything which has happened to me since then has to be traced back to the day he walked in and persuaded me to take on the job as coach at Dens Park. Believe me, it took all his powers of persuasion to talk me into taking on the job. There were several reasons for that. My own lack of confidence definitely held me back from accepting the job — especially as it meant going back to Dundee. My time as a player there had not been happy. Not to put too fine a point on it, the fans hated me. I struggled there more than I did at any other club because they gave me so much stick. Even now the memories of that time hurt. It was probably the one place where I was really unhappy as a player. The other lads at the club were fine. The manager Bobby Ancell was a gem. The fans were the real problem and there was never any way that I could please them.

From the very start they were against me because I had been bought for something like £10,000 from Clyde and arrived there along with the striker Sammy Wilson from Falkirk just after the fans had seen Alan Gilzean leave for Spurs. Inevitably we were compared with Gilzean, and then, when Charlie Cooke left soon after we had been signed, we were compared with him too. I don't think either of us stood a chance because the fans went along to the games looking for the star players and instead of finding them found us — two bargain buys who were never judged on our own merits. If we had simply been bought and joined up with the team we played in and there had been no history of star players being sold by Dundee then we would have been accepted. I'm sure of that. Even more sure of it today than I was then! But the sad thing was that we were never given a break by the supporters. They saw that the stars had gone, looked at us in their places and we were the people there they could take it out on. It made for a very unhappy time for me as a player because I was in a no win situation from the very beginning.

A VISIT CHANGES MY LIFE

The start of Jim McLean's managerial career — when he takes over as coach at Dens Park. Here McLean is welcomed to the job by Dundee's then skipper Doug Houston who is now a member of the Tannadice backroom staff. Other players in the picture are, left to right, — Alex Bryce, Ally Donaldson, John Duncan, Dave Johnston, Joe Gilroy, Dave Soutar, Charlie McVicar and Alex Kinninmonth. (Courtesy of D.C. Thomson.)

Yet I had pushed to get there. Pushed to leave Clyde where John Prentice had been my manager because I wanted the chance of first-team football which Dundee offered me. I was 28 years old when I moved there to start a career as a full-timer. Honestly, I know that Prentice did not want to sell me but I had heard Dundee wanted me. They had made an offer which Clyde turned down, then when I kicked up a fuss about it all they agreed to sell me. It was the attraction of going full time and joining a much bigger club which had made me want to move. Nothing else — because Clyde gave me some of my best times as a player. Probably that's why the reception I got at Dundee in game after game was such a stark contrast for me. I'd never experienced that kind of treatment before and it affected me badly. I think it scarred me for many, many years.

JOUSTING WITH GIANTS

Looking back and remembering these three miserably unhappy seasons I still cannot understand it all completely. Besides the problem of the stars who had gone there was also, I think, my own approach to the game which the fans couldn't — or didn't want to — understand. My philosophy as a player was the same as my philosophy has always been as a coach or a manager. I didn't believe in giving the ball away then and I hammer that into players today as well. It remains the main plank of my thinking as a manager. But it's easier to get the point across as a team boss. As a player I would not pass a ball unless I thought the player who was going to accept that pass was in a good position. Or was unmarked. I would rather keep possession myself than risk losing it by making the wrong pass. So if players were not moving into good positions, then I would keep the ball, possibly be caught in possession myself by an opponent and the crowd would get on top of me. The one thing I'm glad about from that period of my life is that even through all the jeering, all the barracking that I had to take, they were not able to change my thinking. It would have been disastrous for me if I had given in to them and just played the kind of careless ball which might look good to fans on the terracings but means nothing to fellow professionals on the park.

It was during this time, too, that my distrust of the Press grew. Because I was the kind of player I was — not flashy, not the kind of player who went off on runs beating two or three defenders — no one outside the game appreciated what I was all about. The player who beat me could do that and then send a cross over the byeline but still be hailed as a hero. It didn't make sense to me then when I was playing and it doesn't make sense to me now as a manager. It still goes on, believe me. We have young Kevin Gallacher who can do no wrong as far as the fans are concerned. If he falls over the ball the crowd will still love him. On the other hand we had Billy Kirkwood who didn't get anything like the credit he deserved. I remember the games we had against Manchester United in the UEFA Cup a few seasons back. Kirky didn't give Bryan Robson a kick of the ball over the two legs. And he doesn't give the ball away very often either — yet the fans never warmed to him as much as they should have. I still think that's wrong. In fact I felt as upset about that as I did when I was playing myself. The distrust of the Press has faded a little but there are still times when I feel that players and managers look for different things from the game than either the Press or the fans.

Going back to these troubled times at Dens Park, I still believe that I

14

Jim the joiner! This was how Manager McLean liked to relax — building his own homes. This is him at work when he was still a player at Dens Park. (Courtesy of D.C. Thomson.)

did a better job for Dundee than any of the supporters gave me credit for. Over the three seasons I spent with them I think I'm right in saying that I was always either second-top or third-top goal scorer. Never top — but I was scoring goals regularly for the team and I'm still sure that I was a better player than the fans remember. Or are willing to admit.

Anyhow, all of this was still fresh in my mind when I was suddenly asked to go back there as coach. Of all the clubs I had been with — Hamilton, Clyde and, at the time of the offer, Kilmarnock — Dundee was the one I could not imagine going back to. It was an amazing offer because John Prentice was putting his head on the chopping block for me. Apart from my own unwillingness to return I'm sure I would have been the last man on earth that the Dundee support wanted to see back there as a coach. Apart from all of that, I'd never given coaching a thought. I was like any other player — and they are the same today. I would go back in the afternoons at Dens Park and kick a ball about. I used to go back with Alex Hamilton, the international full-back, and we would belt balls about the park. It wasn't doing us any good. We could strike the ball OK, but it was easy and it was enjoyable and that was all that mattered. If I'd been thinking like a coach at that time then I would have been back working on the weaknesses in my game. In my own case I should have been practising heading or brushing up on my tackling, things that were problems for me. But it's typical of players that you do the things that you are good at; instead of working on your weaknesses you spend time on the things that you can do without the slightest problem. It's sloppy thinking and when I was a player I was as guilty of that in training as anyone else.

I don't know what it was John Prentice had recognised in me and it was only when he offered me the job as a coach that I realised that to some extent I had fallen under his spell. You see, he had helped me a great deal as a player in my time with him at Clyde but it was only later that I realised just how important an influence he had been. I had gone to Shawfield from the Acas for £5,000 when Johnny Haddow was manager and Dawson Walker trainer. Then John Prentice took over and he transformed us. He guided the team to fourth place in the First Division. This was Clyde, mind you. Part-time. Unfashionable. Yet he did that and he did it by taking ordinary players, as opposed to outstanding players, and getting them to perform magnificently for the team. Anyone who played there at that time would agree with me. He would take free transfer players or buy someone for maybe £500 and transform them.

The two McLeans who were together at Dens Park. On the left Jim and on the right George, the one time Rangers' star who played alongside the Tannadice boss at Dundee. (Courtesy of D.C. Thomson.)

Myself and Sam Hastings, in particular, were helped under his management. Sam scored 24 goals that season, and I was just one goal behind him, although some of mine came from penalty kicks. Now, you have to remember here that this was Clyde we are talking about. Also this was a left-wing partnership grabbing all these goals between them. I was inside-left and Sam was on the wing and we shared almost 50 goals. It was unbelievable and it was all down to the manager.

When John Prentice left the game it was a heavy, heavy loss for Scottish football even though a lot of people may not have realised that at the time. He didn't get the credit he deserved because there were times when he did not get his message over completely — he was ahead of his time. In many ways I never did fulfil my own potential as a player. If I came close to that at all then it was in that season at Shawfield when he was my manager. His guidance brought me close to the best that I was capable of producing and it's a tragedy that he left the game. You would only have to ask the players who were there at Clyde about him. People like Harry Glasgow, Jim Fraser, Davie Souter, Sam Hastings and myself — he made us better players. His knowledge of the game combined with a very shrewd yet solid management style made it all possible for him. He just had this knack of getting players and fitting them into a team system which suited them and and which suited the team pattern. Without any doubt he was the best manager I ever played for. I don't want to be thought of as being critical of any of the other managers but he was the number one, the major influence in my career.

At Hamilton, Johnny Low was the man who signed me. He was a fruit merchant in the town and he was the man who put me on the road. I still hear about him now and again and manage to keep in touch with how he is doing. I'm always grateful to him for plucking me out of the juniors and giving me a chance in senior football. At Dundee Bobby Ancell, who had bossed Motherwell in their great days when they had Pat Quinn, Ian St John and Willie Hunter and the rest, was a complete gentleman. Again, I owed him the chance I got of going full time at a very late age. It was old then to suddenly become a full-timer at 28 — it would not be possible now when you start chasing players that are just coming out of primary school! Then, at Kilmarnock I had Walter McCrae as manager. Without the slightest doubt he was the best trainer I ever worked under in all my time in the game. He was magnificent at that aspect of the game. My time at Rugby Park was short but it was one of the happiest times for me. Partly, I suppose,

As a player with Dundee, Jim McLean, spent the most miserable time of his soccer career. (Courtesy of D.C. Thomson.)

because it came after the heart-breaking time with Dundee but, also, because my wee brother had been there before me. Honestly, they thought so much of our Tom down there at Rugby Park that I could have been playing on one leg and they would still have welcomed me just because I was his big brother.

It was a wrench to leave there and go back to Dens Park. John Prentice had to work very hard to get me to accept the job. I had misgivings about my own ability to be a coach. That old lack of confidence cropped up again as I thought about his offer. Then, as well as the feud with the fans, I did not have much respect for the directors who were there at the time. So John Prentice had to convince me that I would be answerable only to him and that all my dealings at the club would be with the players and with him. No one else would interfere with that arrangement. Until I had that assurance I was not going to take the job.

Yet, when I went there to take the job, not having a clue where I was going to start or how I was going to handle it, everything seemed to go right. I don't know yet how it happened but I took to the job like a duck to water. There must have been some deep-down instinctive thing which helped me because, honestly, I had never contemplated doing this for a living.

The players helped me over the first hurdles. I realise that now. Most of them had played with me there and knew me and when John Prentice pushed me in at the deep end and told me to start taking the training they knew how nervous I was. It's embarrassing now to think about the training I did then and the way I plan things now. There is no comparison at all. I just didn't know a thing about the job — but it came right. I told the players that first day what I thought about the job and the responsibility that it carried. If I recall correctly I said to them: "The one thing you can be sure of is that whatever I'm thinking I will let you know face to face. I won't hide anything from any of you. Then, at the end of the day, I know that I will get the sack if I'm not good enough. So, from the start I will do things my way." I have never moved from that viewpoint. From the start I think I must have got that credo right because I cannot recall struggling in the job. OK, I had these early nerves and John Prentice didn't come out to help me through. He stayed away from the training and let me get on with it. He seemed to have that kind of confidence in me and in a way that helped me through those early days as coach.

It was a good partnership, the classic double act if you like. I went out on to the training ground and bawled and shouted at the players while he sat in his office as the quiet man of the duo. There were times when I would hit the odd player or two with a fine and I'd tell him and send them in to see him. But to this day I don't know if any of them were ever fined by him.

As a coach across the road at Dens Park I worked the same way as I work now, the difference being that then I was the coach. In that role the players appreciated totally what you were trying to do for them. It's a new ball game when you become a manager. The whole attitude of the playing staff changes. There is no way that you are going to be Mr Popularity if you are a manager. It's then that you have to make the hard decisions. You are the man who drops players. You are the man who fines players. You are the man who transfers players. You are the man who leaves players out of European squads. In essence you become the man who cannot possibly keep everyone happy — but because of the nature of the job you have to try to do just that!

Of course, the other aspect was that I had played alongside most of them before being transferred. Then, even after moving to Kilmarnock, I still trained at Dens Park a couple of times a week. The rest of the time I travelled to Rugby Park. But my home was in Dundee and I worked with the lads I was now coaching. I like to think that the relationship between me and the players was a special one. Gordon Wallace was there and he is my assistant manager at Tannadice now. Dougie Houston was there and he is part of the backroom staff here too. The players were tremendous as well. Jocky Scott, now a rival as Dundee manager, was there. So were Jim Steele, Jim Easton, George Stewart, Iain Phillip and Bobby Wilson. John Duncan, who was appointed Ipswich manager, was another of the players and I can remember some of the things I used to call him at the training sessions. It's easy to remember them because when I left Dens Park to go to Tannadice the players put together a cassette of all the insults I had hurled at them and all the names I'd called them and presented it to me with a cassette recorder. They didn't want me to go and, really, I didn't want to leave them either. That was the happiest spell I ever knew at Dens Park. It helped ease the bitterness I felt over the three seasons as a player. John Prentice did all the right things. He picked the team every week. He went to the board meetings and dealt with the directors. He looked after the financial side of the club. All I had to do was the training and the conditioning and the coaching. It was a remarkably happy time for me.

My view of the game was instinctive, I think. It didn't come particularly through John Prentice and what he preached to us at Clyde, for example. I guess it was there all the time but it was just that I never, ever thought that I would be given the chance of passing on any knowledge to other people. Just to illustrate the point I'm trying to make, I'll tell you a story which Steve Murray told me. He was playing for Aberdeen this day and I was playing for Dundee and the manager at Pittodrie was Eddie Turnbull. During the game Eddie was trying some tactical ploy against us and I could see what it was. I counteracted it. Out there on the field I somehow neutralised whatever it was Aberdeen were trying to do. After the game Turnbull had told the players in the dressing room, "That bandit McLean mucked it up . . .". What he meant was that I'd been able to see what he was attempting and block his moves. That was before I was coaching. Before I considered coaching. Before I had even heard about coaching courses. So there was something there. Eddie Turnbull recognised it. So, thankfully, did John Prentice.

It still rates as a top tribute in my book for Eddie Turnbull to say that about me. I never worked with him as a coach but I would have liked to. Apart from eventually learning from him at the coaching courses at Largs I never had that opportunity. Of all the managers and coaches I came into contact with it remains a regret that I didn't have the chance to work closely with him on a day-to-day basis. In my early days as a manager he was at Hibs and whenever we played them I would be sitting in that dugout waiting and wondering to see what he would come up with. I admired him tremendously. He epitomised the thinking side of the game. The tactical approach was everything to him and, like John Prentice, he was doing that before a whole lot of other managers had appreciated the changes which were taking place in the game.

Like myself Prentice preached that you had to keep possession. I was a very willing disciple. I believed that myself — and with my tackling power there was no way that I could win a lost ball back. I had to try to keep it away from the opposition! So I was on the same wavelength and then when I was looking and learning from other teams and from other countries it was to the West Germans and the Dutch that I went first of all. They had the systems I admired and they had a whole approach to the game which gelled with the ideas I was beginning to formulate for myself. They wanted to make passes. They wanted to keep the ball on the ground and they wanted to play possession football.

When I first arrived at Tannadice as the manager we had a player, a

Debut day for Jim McLean as he takes the field for the first time as a Dundee player — behind him is Charlie Cooke. (Courtesy of D.C. Thomson.)

defender, who used to go into tackles and win the ball and then lump it up on to the terracings. I'm not joking — that was his speciality! Obviously I just couldn't understand this at all. It was not the way I had tried to play the game and it was not the way I wanted to see the game played. There was no point to it, really. It was senseless. Yet that player persisted in playing that way even though all it meant for the team was that after managing to win the ball, to gain possession of the ball, they had to go out and do that all over again. There is no way that a team can ever win games using that kind of approach. But it is one which seems to be adopted by players in different teams at different times. It's wholly alien to my views of football and wholly alien to the way really good teams play the game.

That second spell at Dens Park was so much happier than the years as a player, mainly because of John Prentice, but also because of the new job I had and the players who were there who helped make the job easy. Then I decided to try for the manager's job at Tannadice, not because I was unhappy but because there was a strong rumour going about that John Prentice was leaving Scotland to go to Canada. George Stewart had heard this in Edinburgh and he told me. I believed it. In fact I was upset that Prentice never told me and I knew that if he left I would not stay on. I wouldn't have been able to handle the directors even if they did decide to give me the job as manager. Mind you, it's doubtful if they would have done that. Although I was back working for Dundee my relations with the board had not changed. They knew how I felt about them and only the presence of John Prentice as a buffer between myself and the board kept life sweet for me.

The news about the Canadian business worried me so much that I contacted the United manager Jerry Kerr one Saturday morning and asked him if there was any chance of a job as a coach. We went to Ibrox that day and Dundee beat Rangers — but the die was cast. As far as I was concerned, I had to get another job. As it turned out I made the right move because Davie White came in at Dens Park to take over as manager and I would not have been able to work with him as his number two.

Jerry Kerr came back to me and, in December 1971, I was appointed manager of Dundee United. It was the start of a partnership with the club which is still going on, but it worried me at the time. And these worries have surfaced on and off for the whole time I have been in the job. Even to this day I maintain that I'd be happier as a coach than as a manager. My nature is better suited to the coaching job because as a manager I allow my tension, my nervousness, to transmit itself to the players at times. It's a problem but there are times when I can't prevent it happening. Also the drive for perfection that I have can mean players getting as much stick from me when they have won a game as when they have lost one.

As a coach at Dens Park there was always John Prentice behind me, guiding me or even stepping in to encourage players I had maybe slated. It was the right balance. A perfect team, we were, and we could have continued that. I'd still love just to be working with players and coaching them, rather than making those decisions which present every manager with headaches.

It's probably significant that today I still listen to John Prentice when he offers me advice. He has never advised me wrongly or badly and has easily been the biggest single influence on my career. He might still phone me to give me stick about things I have done wrong — and I'll listen. I'll always listen to him. Without his encouragement and his guidance I would not have lasted half as long in this job as I have done. Without his influence I would be back working as a joiner.

Chapter Two

RANGERS AND THE OFFER I COULD REFUSE

If my mentor John Prentice was able to make me an offer I couldn't refuse when he talked me into becoming his coach at Dens Park there were other offers I could turn down. And I did. Eleven times in my 16 years as manager of Dundee United I have knocked back clubs who wanted me to join them. Not all of the offers have been made public and not all of them tempted me to leave Tannadice. But there were some which tried my loyalty to this club to the limits.

The most highly publicised of them all was when I was offered the Rangers job in the autumn of 1983, only a few months after winning the Premier League championship with United for the first time in the club's history. John Greig had resigned from the Ibrox job, my old sparring partner Alex Ferguson had been offered the job and then, when he turned down the Ibrox club, I was approached and asked to take over. Inevitably the news leaked out and the negotiations and the talks which were supposed to stay so secret and so private almost became a circus. I was caught in the middle of all this, a situation I did not enjoy, because essentially I'm a private person and I would rather have thought things over without the publicity spotlight being trained on me for a whole nerve-wracking weekend.

It was quite easily the worst weekend of my whole life. Because the offer Rangers made to me could not have been bettered anywhere at all. Financially it was the best offer of any of the 11 that I have received — and far and away better than anything that Dundee United might have been able to offer me. In everything else the Rangers directors were ready to give me a free hand. It was a fantastic offer, even better than I would ever have imagined possible. I knew that Rangers were a big, big club. So much bigger than we can ever be at Tannadice. I knew, too, that they desperately wanted success but I didn't realise just how much money they were prepared to pay to get that success. I found out very quickly in my talks with the board.

Quite simply, Rangers offered to buy me a £100,000 house in the West of Scotland. They promised to double the basic salary I had with United. And they guaranteed the same bonuses and pension.

To anyone with the slightest knowledge of football it's obvious, too, that the chance of getting regular bonuses with Rangers is going to be a little bit easier than it is at Tannadice. In my opinion it's far easier to win trophies with them than it is with Dundee United!

But the house could have been the clincher. I had met Jock Stein in the car park at Hampden shortly before I was going to meet the Ibrox directors. I wanted to see him because I knew he would be able to advise me on the kind of salary a Rangers' manager should be getting. I tend to be naïve about these matters despite what some of my critics may think. No one knows my salary at Tannadice apart from myself and the chairman. It has always been that way. The directors don't know it. First of all Johnstone Grant knew it and now George Fox, and I have never asked them for a rise in all the years I have been here. Any increase I have had has come as an offer from them and I've never argued one way or another about money with them.

I reckoned Jock would give me sound advice and he suggested that I should ask about a house because he knew that I was the kind of manager who had to live on the doorstep if I was going to be doing the job properly. If I take on a job then I am going to be totally committed to it. So the first thing I asked about was the house and it seemed to be no problem at all. Then we talked about money and the offer was detailed. It was a fantastic offer. Looking back I still realise that.

Apart from the financial security which the job spelled out for me and for my family the board explained that I would be given a completely free hand as manager of the club. No restrictions would be placed on me whatsoever. In regard to the signing of players it would be done solely on my judgment of the players and there would be no interference from the board at all. That is the same with Dundee

United. It was also going to be the same in any of the other managerial job offers I had had. There is no other way I could take on a job without having total control over the playing side of the club. But to hear this at Ibrox was important. More than just important — it was crucial. What the directors were telling me was that I could sign a Roman Catholic player for the club if that's what I wanted to do. They would not raise any objections.

The then chairman of the club was Mr Rae Simpson, whom I had known from the time I had at Kilmarnock as a player. He had been club doctor there and had treated me for a very bad injury at one time. He led the talks and both he and the other members of the board made it very plain to me that any ban on Catholic players was not a part of club policy. They seemed completely in agreement on this and also on the fact that the whole business of signing Catholic players was no longer important to them. Or to Rangers. It was not an important factor in club policy. They wanted the old mould broken — just as I would have done if I had taken the job.

In fact, it would have been a matter of urgency for me. I would not have been able to do the job with that kind of limitation placed on me. You cannot perform properly if you are being shackled or handicapped. And I saw the non-signing of Catholics down through the years as a definite handicap for Rangers. They were limiting themselves, making it harder for themselves to get players. I accepted then, as I do now, that there is another side to the problem. The whole vexed question has been there for so long now that it would be difficult to get a Catholic player to sign for the club. Would he want the problems which would come from being the first Catholic player at Ibrox? Or would a parent let his son go into that situation in the West of Scotland where religion remains a problem? It is a whole lot more difficult than people imagine. It's too easy simply to say Rangers should go out and sign Catholic players. Who says they want to play for the club? Maybe the best answer to the problem would have been for me to buy two or three top class Roman Catholic players at the one time. That might have been the easiest way of breaking the taboos which plagued the club.

Anyway, all of their plans and their ideas, all of their offers, financial and otherwise, were paraded in front of me that Sunday afternoon at Ibrox. Then they took me out on to the field and let me look at the stadium from there and I knew then that this was the biggest offer I'd had. Maybe the biggest I would ever get. I don't suppose I needed that little tour of Ibrox. I knew how impressive it was and I knew how big the

The day he turned down a fortune to take over as manager of Rangers, Jim McLean still raises a smile as he announces the news that he is remaining at Tannadice. Present chairman George Fox is on the left while the late chairman Johnstone Grant is on the right. (Courtesy of D.C. Thomson.)

job was. I hadn't known until that day just how much they were prepared to pay to the man they wanted and how much power they were ready to give him. As it turned out I was going to get the same total authority over the playing side as I had with United, but at double the money. With that £100,000 house there was an added bait.

Yet, just under 24 hours later, I had turned down the whole marvellous package. There are still times when I think back to that offer and I regret the decision I made — but I was placed in an extraordinarily complicated situation. Anyone who knows me well recognises that any decision I have to make can turn out to be complicated. This one didn't need my own complex reasoning to be that way. It started out with my being pulled in all sorts of different directions by the different loyalties and ambitions which came into play over the few days I had to make up my mind.

I had loyalty to Dundee United, especially a deep personal loyalty to my chairman, Johnstone Grant. That exerted a tremendous influence on me to stay with Dundee United. On the other hand, my younger brother Tommy was at Ibrox where he had been assistant manager to John Greig and he had been carrying on as caretaker boss. If I went there he would have stayed in a job as long as he wanted to. It would have been part of my accepting the job that Tommy stayed in some capacity or another. If I didn't go to Rangers then it was odds-on that he would lose his job.

I saw it as a black and white choice. I had to knife my brother or knife the chairman. Maybe others wouldn't have seen it in that way. My view, though, brought it all down to that. It was a terrible dilemma for me although eventually I elected to knife Tommy and felt dreadful about doing it. Fortunately it worked out well for him because he was appointed manager of Morton and then soon moved on to be manager of Motherwell.

It would have been harder for the chairman to recover in the same way. I'm not exaggerating my own importance to the club when I say that it would have broken his heart. In many, many ways he treated me like a son and I knew that he was ill at the time. I just didn't know how seriously ill he was. It was only a few months later that he died. If I had left the club and that had happened I would have still been blaming myself. I continue to feel mixed up about the whole business but I did make the right decision as regards my relationship with the chairman, and also out of loyalty to the club who had given me my chance as a manager and who had stayed loyal to me down through the years — even when there were troubled times. That was important, and just as important was my family.

Driving back to Dundee that night, it hit me just how much my wife and two sons would be affected by any moves away from the city. We would be separated for a year, even with that house offer which Rangers had made me. My two sons were at difficult stages as regards their education. One was finishing a college course and the other one was finishing school. There was no way that we would be able to move them from Dundee at that period. It would have been unfair to them and living apart would have been a nightmare for me, though I suppose for the seven or eight months it would have been necessary I would have survived. But I didn't know how they would have liked that change. They were happy in Dundee. We had had a good family life in the city and the boys had grown up there. It would be a wrench for them to leave and so all of that came into consideration.

Of course, I had put extra pressure on myself by placing a deadline

The kind of family atmosphere Jim McLean claims he would have missed if he had moved to Rangers. Here his son Gary clutches the League Cup after United's victory over Aberdeen at Dens Park. (Courtesy of D.C. Thomson.)

on my decision. I had promised Rangers that I would let them know within 24 hours of my meeting with them. They didn't ask me to do that. It was self-imposed and it made the agony greater for me. I had always known that the chairman would take it badly if I thought of leaving. He had known of the other offers and he had been able to talk me round because not all of the offers tempted me. This time I was tempted. More than ever before. And Johnstone Grant knew that. So did the other directors.

Over the few days from the opening approach by Rangers, who handled all of the negotiations magnificently, until my meeting with the Ibrox board I was under pressure. The directors at Tannadice were in tears at the thought of my going. The chairman phoned me constantly and every conversation ended with him crying over the phone. He sent flowers and chocolates to my wife and he pointed out how much I'd meant to the club. Apart from that, I knew what the club had meant to me — yet in a way it was the right time to leave if I was going to leave. A few months earlier we had won the Premier League and while we were now waiting for the quarter-final of the European Cup I knew that it is often the time to walk away from a club — when you have had success. And when you know how difficult it will be to repeat that success. In my opinion it is much harder for a manager to stay with the same club for year after year than it is to keep moving on. A new club brings new challenges. You have new surroundings, new players and the adrenalin begins pumping again. When you are at the same club for a long time you miss some of the things which managers thrive on. It's hard to come into the same ground for 15 or 16 years, looking at so many of the same players in the same dressing-room on the same training ground and going through the same ritual day after day. In many ways it was the time to go.

As far as Jim McLean, football manager, was concerned I made the wrong decision to stay with Dundee United. I should have gone to Rangers. No one will ever convince me otherwise. I have absolutely no doubts about that at all.

But Jim McLean, football manager, is not the sole factor in my life. It's not even the most important factor. All the other feelings came into play — my family and my chairman and my feelings for United. Selfishly, looking only at myself and at my job and at the career prospects which were on offer, I was a fool to turn down Rangers. On the other level, as Jim McLean, individual, then I was right. But even in saying that there is no point in trying to con people or mislead people and say that the decision and the offer I had never cross my mind. On many, many sleepless nights and on many, many other occasions I do wish that I had taken on the Rangers' job. I wasn't frightened by the size of it because I genuinely feel that the job I have to do at Tannadice is a harder job. I'm certain that I could do the job that Graeme Souness has now — though probably not in the same way — but I don't know if he could do my job here at Tannadice. I'm not being disrespectful to Graeme Souness in saying that. I admire what he has done at Rangers and his first season successes in the Skol Cup and the Premier League were outstanding achievements. But different problems exist with this club and it is a long, long time since Graeme will have encountered the kind of worries that exist outside the major teams.

I believe that I have one of the most difficult and demanding jobs in the country — but it is also a richly rewarding and satisfying job when things have gone right. It has been good for me because I look at the financial handicaps and the limited resources which we have and then see that we are still able to challenge the two biggest clubs in the country in Rangers and Celtic. We don't have the resources that they have but for a long time now we have been able to challenge them. And at times beat them! Apart from the Old Firm every club in the country can look at us and identify with us. They can see the problems we have and understand them because they have the same problems. When we win something then maybe it can act as an example to all of them. Because if we can do it then other small clubs can surely do it too. Rangers and Celtic live apart from that. Their crowds insulate them from the problems of survival which hit other clubs. But beating these worries makes you feel good. It makes the struggle worth while!

Maybe, of course, it was not the right time to go. Maybe God gave me the right decision when I was walking into Tannadice that Monday morning still not knowing whether I was staying or not. When Graeme Souness received the offer from Ibrox it was the right time to go there. I never got the offer then and didn't expect to get it again because I had turned them down and I don't think Rangers are the kind of club who would go back to someone who had rejected them. I know that I don't like doing that as a manager. I don't like going back to players to make them offers after they have turned me down earlier.

Deep down it was right for me as a person to give up the chance of the bigger stage I would have had at Ibrox. You sometimes wonder how you would have handled all the pressure which goes with the job, though many of the frustrations you have to handle with a small club would have been gone. That would have balanced the books to some extent.

I was in the house on the day that the news came over the radio that Jock Wallace had been sacked. I remember turning to my wife and saying, "You know, that could have been me?" I think that it might have been me if I had taken the job because I don't know if the Rangers fans would have had the patience to allow me to do the job the way I would have wanted to do it. It would not have been in my nature to go in there and do the job with the flamboyance and the confidence of Graeme Souness. I would have tried to do it the way I have worked here and I don't know that they would have been prepared for that. They want success all the time. They want to be winning games every week and to do that you need ready-made players — as Graeme Souness saw very early on.

Young players cannot do the job for a team nowadays as early as they did when the old First Division was in existence. Then you could push players into the first team at 17 and know that they would be able to play for you that season. I did it with people like Andy Gray. I couldn't do it now even with the exceptional players. You have had two or three years added on before players are ready to come into your team. The demands of the Premier League make it that way. So a youth policy, which is the foundation of any club's success in my opinion, takes an awful lot longer to come to fruition. The Ibrox support would not have allowed me that amount of time. For Jock Wallace sacked, you could have read Jim McLean sacked in the headlines!

Among the other jobs I was offered was that as manager of Hearts — and that came twice. Again I was tempted because when the second offer arrived I was genuinely becoming disheartened at the crowds we were able to attract to Tannadice. We were building a team which was of a very high standard but the support was not available the way it would have been at Tynecastle. Outside the Old Firm, Hearts have the best base for building a top team. They get tremendous support and I do envy them that. It was the factor which almost took me to Tynecastle.

Then I had offers from Motherwell — and they came on three different occasions. I was also asked to take over as manager of Chelsea, then as manager of Wolves when they were still a First Division club. West Ham asked me to join John Lyall as his assistant manager, but being number two didn't have the same attraction by that time as it might have had earlier. And there was also an offer to take

RANGERS AND THE OFFER I COULD REFUSE

Jim McLean, his wife Doris and son Gary all look delighted that the United manager has decided to stay with the Tannadice team — this was the day he turned down the chance to go to Rangers. (Courtesy of D.C. Thomson.)

over Toronto Blizzards and that almost took me across the Atlantic because I believed that the game could take off there and it would have been good to be a part of it all. Then, in the season when we went to the UEFA final I was offered the job of manager with Hibs. The chairman at Easter Road contacted me after John Blackley had resigned from the job and he gave me a very good offer. It was tempting too. Financially, it was better than I was getting at Tannadice but, again, I stayed put.

Now I'll be staying with United until it's time to give up the job — and that date is not far off. It won't be in the too distant future that I decide to take a back seat. I'm a director of the club, of course, and I may stay on in that capacity if I feel I can make any kind of contribution from the board room. But I'm not tempted to take on a lot of power at this club or at any other. I think that directors are crazy to take the stick they get. It must be great to be a director of a club when it is going well, even to own a club when it is highly successful, but the heartbreaks when things go wrong are something else.

I don't have the power at Tannadice that outsiders believe I possess. This club has always been run 100 per cent by the board of directors. The real power has been wielded by the chairman of the club in my time as manager. First of all it was Johnstone Grant, now it is George Fox, and that is how it should be. The financial power, the real clout, has to lie with them. I have enough to do organising the training, laying down the tactics and generally running the team. The finances are handled directly by the board. They deal with the players' contracts and they even settle the bonus payment for every game 24 hours before the match is played. On a Friday, for instance, the weekly board meeting is held at Tannadice and that's when the directors decide what kind of bonus should be on offer to the players for the game the following day. For 12 years — before I was appointed a director — I had very little to do with that. That is the way it should be. Why should I want to saddle myself with that kind of problem when I have enough problems of my own handling, training and coaching the players?

It's been good over the years and that is why I have been content to stay. The club has been good for me — and good to me. I would have made more money going to Rangers. My future, financially, would have been assured. But I could still have been given the sack. This club has a loyalty to me. All I have done is return that loyalty. In the end that is as important as any £100,000 house and any kind of "double your money" offer.

I'm grateful to Rangers that they offered me the job. Knowing that other people want you helps boost your confidence and that's a commodity that I've always been short on. As for Dundee United — well, they are going to have to put up with me for another year or two. But not much longer. I'll know when it is time to move out of the job and already I sense that it is coming close. I won't go anywhere else. Not now. I don't think I would want to. This club gave me something very important — a manager's job when no one else would have wanted me. And the platform to build a team which has been able to bring success to Tannadice. The years have been hard. They have been demanding. They have also been the most rewarding years of my life. Money couldn't buy that.

Chapter Three

BRUTALITY IN THE PREMIER LEAGUE

It's scarcely a secret that I don't enjoy the Premier League set-up and the pressures which it places on clubs. I've maintained for a long time that the cut-throat atmosphere which exists makes managers and coaches and players — the people whose jobs depend on staying in the League — more defensively minded than they should be. I've been that way myself. You are forced into a survival game at some stage of your time in the top division because the stakes are so high. I still think that the players who have been here with me since the start of the Premier League have been affected by the caution I had to show in the early days. It was essential that we stayed in the top ten then and there were chances we might have slipped out. If we had done that there is no saying how long that slip would have lasted. We could have slid all the way down into obscurity and I felt that very strongly.

The Premier League means that we are competing with the top teams, that our supporters are seeing the best teams in the country and that we have a chance of European football season after season. Yet all of this comes with a price. A heavy price! I happen to believe that the Premier League in Scotland is the most physical, cynical and brutal league in the world. I mean that. You hear people talk about wild tackling in Spain or in some of the other Latin countries. I don't think any of their hatchet men would be able to live with some of those in our

League. I know that people will question my views on this. They'll take a look at what I'm saying and reckon there is a motive behind the remarks. They will suggest that I'm trying to protect Paul Sturrock or Kevin Gallacher. It's not true. I'm only trying to protect the game as a whole.

The people want to come to football matches to be entertained and therefore the players they want to watch are the creative players. The fans love skill, imagination and flair. They like to see the top players demonstrate the ability they have. They look for good passes being made, or players making good runs with the ball or scoring the kind of goal that will have everyone talking after the game. That's natural. It's good that the fans want to see all of these things. But, equally, we as managers and coaches should be prepared to allow them to see skill and applaud it.

Somehow we fall down in our duty to the paying customer — because we want to play negatively. We want to stop the good players and to do that we encourage lesser players who may be more efficient. Of course it's always easier to destroy than to create. Also it takes far less time. Creating something is always going to take longer and is always going to need much more time spent in perfecting the finished product. But I always look at this whole question the way I would look at building a house — or knocking one down. It is a whole lot easier to knock it down. That takes no time at all compared to the months and months of hard work needed to build the house. Football is the same . . . and sadly coaches encourage it.

Paul Sturrock or Kevin Gallacher or Gordon Strachan, when he was with Aberdeen, or Charlie Nicholas, when he was at Celtic — they are all players who need protection. But they are not the most important people in this debate and I'm not important at all in the broad picture. The really important thing is the game and right now the whole of football is suffering from the kickers' charter which exists in the Premier League. The tackle from behind is still being used to either intimidate or stop players. Brutal tackling goes on week after week in game after game and often the most cynical challenges of all come on the orders of the manager. I know that certain managers will order players to go out on to the field and boot opposing players in the first few minutes of the game. The reasoning behind that order is simple as well as cynical! It's rare to see anyone being ordered off by a referee as early in a game as that. Even a caution won't always be given in the opening minutes. Also the message has been put over early to the

A pensive McLean as he ponders over tactics for a game. (Courtesy of D.C. Thomson.)

victim. He has been warned. If he hasn't been badly hurt by that tackle, then there will be more to follow.

That's the kind of thing which goes on in Scotland. The kind of thing which, frankly, sickens me of the Premier League. It is damaging to the game because the front players know they are under threat in almost every match. They know that they are going out there on to the field to be kicked up and down by defenders for 90 minutes — if they can hold out that long — and maybe take evasive action.

Strachan and Nicholas must have been delighted to get away from the tactics which were used against them. I know that Paul Sturrock has seriously considered asking for a transfer several times from my own club. When he has done so it has been because he is fed up with the constant intimidation which goes on. He has been a target for more than ten years now and he has picked up injuries which only the front players appear to get regularly.

Until the kind of kicking I am talking about has been removed then we will struggle to get good front players. All of us watched Porto in the European Cup final when they defeated Bayern Munich and we saw the forward play they showed that night. Marvellous, penetrating, individual skills — the kind the public like to see. But how can we develop that kind of player when he is being hacked down at the first opportunity by a defender who has been told "Kick so and so!"?

We have lost our way in Scotland. It seems to be the modern trend in life as a whole that people want to take the easy option in everything and it has become the same in football. It's easier to take a step back in football, especially since the extra defender came into the game. There has been that extra place at the back, an extra place for a defender which has to be filled. So one player is taken away from the front to take over in midfield — and there are never enough places to accommodate the players who want to make the move further back the field. It's a negative viewpoint and it has damaged the game considerably. Yet it's hard to blame some of the players for wanting to come out of the firing line, to move away from that front area where they are going to be hurt.

The risk is there in any League for the forward to get stick. This has to be accepted, I suppose. But in our League it is not so much a risk as a certainty. This is wrong. It used to be an unwritten rule among referees that in any case of doubt then the defender should have the edge. It is not right to think that way now. The game is loaded against the forwards too much as it is. This has to be changed, because it is only when we get back to having forwards who are ready to take on

Letters of good luck which came from all over Britain to Tannadice and Dundee United boss Jim McLean during their glory run to the final of the UEFA Cup against the Swedish team Gothenburg. (Courtesy of D.C. Thomson.)

defenders and run at them with the ball that we will get back to the game the way it is meant to be played. Not just the way it should be played — the way the public want to see it played. Pele called it "the beautiful game" and yet we scar it and deface it by allowing genuinely creative players to be hammered by opponents with less ability.

I accept that some of my colleagues and myself have to carry some responsibility for this sorry mess we are in. Anyone who sends a player out to deliberately kick another is not doing the game a service. Equally the referees have a duty to protect the ball players and in so doing protect the game itself. If referees do not give that protection then let them be suspended the way anyone else can be suspended by the Scottish Football Association.

I know that the SFA have tried to stamp out the kind of tackle I am talking about. They want to get rid of the ruthlessness which ruins the game, but they have not done enough in my opinion. Referees are being asked to look for the diver, for the player who makes tackles look maybe worse than they are. Or to look for a player who is feigning injury to get an opponent in trouble. OK, players who do that are wrong — but the biggest villains in the game are the kickers. They are the ones who cause damage. Does it really make a lot of difference to the game if a diver gets the extra foul or two? I don't happen to think so. But if someone who kicks opponents regularly gets away with it then the game suffers. At the end of the day, in the present set of circumstances, those defenders get more protection than anyone. That is where the real problem lies.

It is a problem which won't be solved by get-togethers between managers and referees. I have not been to the last two meetings, but I was there before and consider it a waste of time. I see it as a cosmetic exercise, something which gives some good publicity about how everyone in the game is working together towards the same objectives and all the rest. It's not true. We have different problems and different views of the same problems. At the meetings I attended the referees spent all their time complaining about managers and how badly we behaved in dugouts. On the other side all we did as managers was moan about the lack of consistency in refereeing decisions. I cannot think of one solitary factor to come out of any of these meetings which has helped solve the major problems in the game.

It breaks my heart to see referees who are more concerned about their own dignity on the field than the mayhem which can sometimes be going on round about them. They will order off a player who looks at

"New Firm" managers Jim McLean of Dundee United and Alex Ferguson, then of Aberdeen, with awards from the SFA for their services at the association's coaching classes. Behind them is former Aberdeen and Manchester United star Martin Buchan. (Courtesy of D.C. Thomson.)

JOUSTING WITH GIANTS

The Premier League title has just been won by Dundee United for the first time and Manager Jim McLean is lifted high on the shoulders of his celebrating players at the end of the game against Dundee at Dens Park. (Courtesy of D.C. Thomson.)

them the wrong way or they will send a manager to the stand from the touchline if he has shouted to question one of their decisions. Meanwhile the real villains can stay on the field wrecking the game.

Something has to be done to change all of that. If not, then we will continue to suffer from the lack of front players. It has been a perennial problem for the international side over the past ten years or so and it will remain a problem until the men who are brave enough to play up front find referees brave enough to hammer the hard men who are slowly but surely destroying the game I love.

Mind you, the referees would need support too and I don't think they get the proper backing from the current system of supervision which exists to assess their performances. I'm not liable to win any popularity poll run by the referees — there is no way that I'm one of their favourite managers. Yet I do think they can get a raw deal at times from the reports which are filled in regarding their performances. They have the supervisors in the stand doing their Big Brother act and

BRUTALITY IN THE PREMIER LEAGUE

they then have managers who are asked to fill in a report after every game. I think both ideas are wrong.

I would abandon the present system of supervisors. In some cases you have former referees who have not been as good as the men they are being asked to judge sitting there deciding how they are running the game. That cannot be right. Nor can it be right that I am asked to send in a report on a referee who might have given a controversial decision

A familiar scene some years ago as McLean finds himself in trouble with a referee during a game at Tannadice. Now he says he has calmed down. (Courtesy of D.C. Thomson.)

against us which has cost the game. That is certain to influence me — it's only human nature and I'm certain every other manager in the country would feel the same. I fill it up every Monday but I'm fairly sure that no one ever pays the slightest bit of attention to it. Why should they? But I do believe that a great deal of attention is paid to the supervisors — and they can finish a referee's career quite easily. I don't think it's right they they should be under pressure from Big Brother in the stand every week or so. I doubt if that can help them. I know it would not help me and it could very well shatter a man's confidence if he thinks that every move is being monitored.

I would prefer it if they said to the top referees, the recognised top group, that they were the best and they just had to go out and get on with it. I think the referees were much more relaxed in the past. You could talk to them and they could talk to you and you could find common ground without the book having to be pulled out. Now the only referees who will speak to you are the ones who are safe, those who are on the FIFA list, say. If you utter the slightest word to some of the younger ones then you find yourself booked and being hauled in front of the Referee Committee. That happens because they are frightened men. Frightened by the supervisors, in my view!

I accept that there is a case for some kind of supervision of officials. There have to be assessments made of younger referees who are looking for promotion. It's the one way they can break through. But I'd like to see it done by ex-players or ex-managers. People who have been through it all themselves and who know the problems from the professional point of view. There are men still around in Scotland who have been discarded far too early by the game and who are still capable of making a contribution. Let men such as John Prentice, Eddie Turnbull, Bobby Seith and others take a look at referees and assess their performances. Let outside people do it rather than keep it only among ex-referees. I believe that they would be fairer and more constructive and let's forget all about asking managers to give their views. That is the biggest joke of all.

Something has to be done to get it over to the referees that the game is suffering from the ruthlessness which has become an integral part of our Premier League. Any manager who condones it — and there are some — is cheating himself and the game. Any referee who allows it is equally guilty. They have the ultimate power. They can order off any player they think is breaking the laws of the game quite deliberately. Vicious tackling against someone who is recognised as a ball player

More trouble for Manager McLean here as he puts his point forcibly to a referee at half time. (Courtesy of D.C. Thomson.)

This used to be a regular occurrence for Dundee United boss Jim McLean — a visit to the SFA offices and a meeting of the Referee and Disciplinary Committee. (Courtesy of D.C. Thomson.)

should be stamped out immediately. If it happens early in the game then rest assured that has been a deliberate ploy on many, many occasions. They shouldn't take into account when it happens — they should only involve themselves with *how* it happens. If it would merit an ordering off in the 73rd minute then it should still merit an ordering off in three minutes!

I genuinely believe that if something is not done to stamp out the brutal tackles we see so often then the game will go into decline. It is heading in that direction now. To change things referees — and managers — must allow the entertainers the opportunity to entertain.

JIM McLEAN BOOK

Chapter 4

TOPPLING THE GIANTS

It's a strange thing, but in the season we reached the final of the UEFA Cup, our run towards Gothenburg brought us more fame, more recognition than we had ever had before because of our wins in Europe over Barcelona and Borussia Moenchengladbach. Yet in all the years we have been playing in the Continental competitions I have found it hard for this club to compete in that arena. There were times when I honestly wondered if it was worth our while even going into the tournaments. Even more than in Scotland where we have less resources than Rangers or Celtic I felt we were the corner shop team playing against the supermarkets of soccer. How can a club as small as Dundee United, with an average gate of less than 10,000, take on Barcelona whose season ticket sales are close to 100,000 every season?

Until that clash when we defeated the Spanish side I was not convinced that we needed Europe. Now I know that we do. Since that win and the follow-up victory over the West Germans in the semi-final of the tournament our club has been recognised across the world. It's not just in Europe that people know us — it's everywhere football is played. And so I realised that no other platform is available to us which can compare with the one offered by Europe.

Perhaps my earlier thoughts were clouded by the financial pressures placed on the club. We seemed to find ourselves drawn regularly

After the match verdict from Dundee United boss Jim McLean as Ian St John interviews him after the Tannadice win over Barcelona in the UEFA Cup quarter-final. (Courtesy of D.C. Thomson.)

against teams from Eastern Europe. That meant long hauls to Rumania or Yugoslavia. To Poland or to Hungary. Bad enough from the playing point of view when players had to suffer long hours in a plane and on some occasions long, long hours in a bus as well. But completely disastrous from a financial standing when the club had to pay out hefty charter air fares, knowing that the clubs you were meeting would not draw big gates at Tannadice. It was a constant nagging worry for me and for the directors of the club and it only altered in recent years, in particular when we faced Barcelona, Borussia and then Gothenburg in the two-legged final. There we made money. Bigger money than we had ever expected!

Strengthening the structure of the club was important for all of us, but the boost that our performances gave us might have been equally important. Apart from the cash side of the situation I began to believe that I had a team at Tannadice who were capable of winning one of the major European competitions. It's always been at the back of my mind that Dundee United should only enter for trophies that we have a chance of winning. At least a reasonable chance! Yet for far too long I did not believe that we had the slightest chance of winning anything at all in Europe. So that, plus the financial headaches, had me constantly doubting the value of the whole exercise.

Now, however, I know we cannot afford to be out of Europe. Not for the money — though it was good in our biggest games — but for the prestige that a run in one of the tournaments can provide for any club. The sad thing is that we cannot guarantee 20,000 crowds for all the ties we play. We could do that for Barcelona and for Gothenburg. We almost did it for the Borussia game . . . but in the earlier rounds against Lens from France, Universitatea Craiovia from Rumania and Hajduk Split of Yugoslavia we pulled in a total for the three home games of just under 34,000 fans. In one of these ties there was a loss of £15,000 made before we hit the quarter-final jackpot with our match against Barcelona.

Don't get me wrong here. I'm not in any way complaining about the supporters who do come to Tannadice for these games. They look for European football every season and they look for us having a fairly lengthy run in whatever tournament we happen to be playing in. It's a bonus for them and they deserve that. I just wish there were more of them. Because more fans coming through the turnstiles would make certain that we could compete with the top teams on more equal terms.

Basically I shudder to think what our gates might slump to if we did not have the stimulus of European football each season. Our fans expect us to be in Europe. They almost demand that we are one of the Scottish clubs playing on the Continent — and I think, too, because we have had some little success they look for us reaching the late rounds. That is certain to be a worry for us in the coming seasons because then we may be on a sticky wicket regarding the quality of players we have here at the club.

Some of our best players are coming to the end of their careers and it's doubtful if we can replace them with people of similar quality. Doing that is becoming more and more difficult. Some of our top players arrived here during a two to three year period and they formed the backbone during the successful times we have enjoyed. I'm talking of Paul Hegarty, Dave Narey, Paul Sturrock and some who left such as Andy Gray, Raymond Stewart and Davie Dodds. Since these golden days we have had the odd players sneaking through to establish themselves in the team — Maurice Malpas is one example while two others who have left, Richard Gough and Ralph Milne, are others. It's when you compare the amount of players we had breaking through in

TOPPLING THE GIANTS

A night of glory in West Germany and scorer Iain Ferguson and Manager McLean salute the Tannadice fans who went to Moenchengladbach for the UEFA Cup semi-final when Dundee United beat Borussia 2-0.

the early years and the amount we have had since that you start to become edgy about the club's future. There are far more clubs active in chasing the young players, especially in Dundee and the surrounding towns where we used to have things all our own way.

Anyhow, that's a worry for the future. The marvellous thing just now is that the club gained such projection from the efforts we made in Europe against Terry Venables' team, Barcelona, and the West Germans who were strongly tipped to take the UEFA Cup. I was happy with the performances in these two games even though the most perfect performances we have given in Europe were against Standard Liege in the second round of the European Cup. I will deal with that match — and that campaign — in another chapter.

Barcelona was not as good a performance but it was probably more enjoyable because of the way it put the club on the map. I'm under no illusions about that, incidentally. It happened because the Spanish side had a powerful British connection which meant that the TV companies and the newspapers were more interested than if we had been playing, say, Real Madrid. Barcelona had Terry Venables as their manager. They had Gary Lineker, the hero for England in the World Cup finals in Mexico, as their main striker. And alongside him they had an old opponent of our defence in Mark Hughes, the Welsh international player who had played against us for Manchester United two years earlier.

Apart fom the publicity aspect it was a formidable line-up we were being asked to take on. As well as that highly rated, highly priced trio, of course, there was a strong scattering of Spanish international players through the team. Nevertheless, it was a quarter-final draw I welcomed. We all knew it would be difficult but we also recognised that it would be the kind of game which would lift our players, provide the fans with the kind of glamour that only Europe can bring, and push the club into the spotlight. Also, at the back of my mind I had a sneaking feeling that we could upset the Spaniards. I didn't think they would relish playing us at Tannadice, a ground where the crowd is almost on top of you, when they were used to the huge Nou Camp Stadium. There was a possibility that could be a problem for us but I was fairly confident that my own players would not be overawed too much by being asked to play there. It would be then, I hoped, that all their European experience would carry them through.

We had played three games in the competition before being drawn against the Spanish aces. Our first round game against Lens was one which promised to be difficult for us, mainly because of the upsurge in French football. Their national team had won the European

TOPPLING THE GIANTS

Dave Narey closes in to tackle Mark Hughes in the Barcelona game at Tannadice.

Championships two years before, and in Mexico they had been hailed for their attacking play and their exciting approach to the game. If that had rubbed off on their club sides then Lens would provide problems.

They did. Yet we were able to overcome these. In the first match — away from home on their Felix Bollaert ground — we lost 1-0. Yet, although we had late escapes ourselves in that match, we also had two scoring tries disallowed by the Austrian referee. Both Paul Sturrock and Kevin Gallacher had the ball in the French net only to see it fail to count. Still, even though we had not scored a valuable goal away from home, it was a sound enough result with the second leg to come at Tannadice. There, two weeks later, goals from Ralph Milne and

JOUSTING WITH GIANTS

Tommy Coyne, in a three-minute spell in the second half pushed us into the second round — but it had been a worrying tie for us.

The next round saw us behind the Iron Curtain, almost inevitably, and it did nothing to help my apprehension when we were drawn to play at Tannadice first. That is never a situation I welcome though it worked fine for us in the next three rounds as well.

Again the game presented us with worries — worries that so often come with tricky European ties. There is always a need for patience in these games and this match was no exception to that general rule. It was the second half before we were able to break down their defence and the last ten minutes before we managed to give ourselves the cushion of goals that we wanted so badly to take with us to Rumania. Ian Redford scored first just after half time, then John Clark scored ten minutes from the end and it was Redford once more who grabbed the third goal in the dying minutes of the match.

Going to Craiovia we were without the men who had been our major defensive stalwarts over our years in Europe, Paul Hegarty and Dave Narey. But even without them we won comfortably enough to then find ourselves faced with another Iron Curtain journey to Split in Yugoslavia where we had to meet Hajduk. At Tannadice we won 2-0 with goals from Jim McInally and John Clark who was becoming a specialist European scorer. The return was a 0-0 draw — and the stage was set for a clash with one of the Continent's bigger names.

We were in the last eight now and were the only Scottish team left in Europe. That was something we had achieved several times before and I still consider it a tribute to the way we approach the games and the meticulous planning we put into them all. When the draw was made and we found ourselves paired with Barcelona we knew that this was the biggest game of all for the club. We had played them before, some 20 years earlier, when United made their first appearance in Europe in the same tournament, which was then called the Fairs Cup. Then Barcelona were holders and United managed to beat them in both games. It was a memory which lingered on for our older fans and for director Doug Smith who had played for the team then. But we all knew that victories cannot come from nostalgia. Memories of two famous wins weren't going to be enough to tame the current Barcelona outfit.

There was another thing I recognised going into the match — that Terry Venables would have them tactically alert. He had won the Spanish League title with them, taken them to the European Cup final

The multi-million pounds Barcelona strike force in action at Tannadice. Here Mark Hughes watches as Gary Lineker misses a chance for the Spanish giants.

the season before and had obviously grafted some British traits on to the usual Latin approach. Venables was a coach I had always admired. I had watched the teams he had had at Crystal Palace and Queens Park Rangers. On other occasions I had seen how he handled the England Under-21 team when he was helping coach them. He put in a lot of work, he seemed to have the kind of vision of the game which I had myself and he always had his team trained particularly well for set pieces. So much so that I have to admit that there were a few of his free kicks I'd seen that I stole and used myself at Dundee United. Little moves that he had perfected and that I'd seen on television were now being used by us. At Tannadice we spend a great deal of time on free kicks and while we work most of them out ourselves I'm never above copying one from someone else if I believe they will work for the team. These ones did and coming up to the game I made no secret of my admiration for Venables.

Nor did I hide my feelings about Lineker and Hughes. My

admiration for the two was genuine — but I felt, also, that it suited my players to know that they were going in against top men whose play and whose style they were familiar with. Mention a Spanish player to them and they would have been alert enough. Mention Lineker and Hughes and you could bet that they would know all about them. The coverage of First Division games and the coverage of Barcelona since the two players had gone there made that certain. Sure, Dundee United had still to get out there over two games and master them, but psychologically I was sure that the players would be in the right frame of mind for the crunch when it came.

Fortunately for us that was more than you could say for Barcelona who were under pressure from their demanding fans. Their home form had slumped. They had not been forgiven for failing to defeat Steaua Bucharest in the final of the European Cup in Seville the previous season. Terry Venables himself was under fire — and Mark Hughes was being pilloried by the Spanish media. In contrast to all of that we had a backing from our media which I appreciated deeply.

For a long, long time I distrusted the Press, possibly because as a player I was never really liked by the newspapermen and so I didn't have a lot of time for them either. As a manager you have to deal with journalists more because of the nature of the job and even then I found it one of the more difficult aspects. All I wanted to do was coach players and train players and talking to the newspapers about the team or the game didn't seem an important part of the job. Jock Stein changed my view of that. Working alongside Jock with the Scotland international squad and seeing just how much effort he had to put in on that side of things taught me a lesson, particularly in the weeks we spent in Spain at the 1982 World Cup finals. The demands made on Jock were enormous — but all of them had to be met. Television, radio, Scottish journalists, foreign journalists — they all had jobs to do and part of that job was speaking to the Scotland manager.

At club level it is not as big, not as intense, but it still has to be done. In our case when we were playing Barcelona we found the sympathetic coverage from the media helped us. While Barcelona were battling with their own Press we were given no problems. Our players were being praised for reaching the quarter-finals while poor Terry Venables was having to deal with questions which asked him to axe Hughes and bring back Steve Archibald. That seemed to be more of an issue at their St Andrews HQ than their first-leg game against us on the day of their arrival.

TOPPLING THE GIANTS

This time John Clark is the Tannadice defender who steps in to clear the danger with Hughes again lurking in the background.

It was easy to see that there was so much more pressure on them. Pressure about the team selections ... pressure about Terry Venables' tactics ... pressure about Mark Hughes' future. In a complete turnabout, we were the opposite of all of that. If we lost then basically few people would have hammered us because there we were, a little team playing against these Spanish giants. If we won then it would be hailed as a major triumph for us and for the whole of Scottish football, because the whole of Scotland was behind us — maybe even the whole of Britain because English clubs remained banned from European competition. We were there carrying the banner for everyone and I like to think that the footballing public took us to their hearts. I thanked the media at the end of that year for the way they had treated the team and for the publicity they had given the club. I meant it too!

Anyhow, there were Barcelona with all their problems and we had only the one major worry — whether we could risk Paul Hegarty or not against the Barcelona strikers. And whether we should use a trio of central defenders against the two million pound men who had been sold from the English First Division in the summer. Hegarty had been out for months and was just getting back to peak fitness. Eventually, just before the match, we decided not to risk him and not to try the three men at the heart of the defence. We thought the risk would be too great in each case.

Before the game I did my best to build up our own players, trying to lift their confidence and trying, also, to give them public credit for what they had already achieved. I stressed that I wanted to have the fans at the ground and those watching on television to end the night talking about our players instead of about the big money buys of Barcelona. It was something I hoped for desperately in the days before the game. When Kevin Gallacher scored a marvellous goal after only two minutes then my prayers began to be answered. That was all the reward we had that night in the first leg, but it was Gallacher's goal and Paul Sturrock's runs which captured the imagination of the millions of fans watching the game on television. While we would have liked more goals we did have one and we had prevented Barcelona from getting a crucial goal away from home. That was of almost equal importance to us as the goal we scored. When matches can hinge on the away goals counting double rule you cannot afford to let one slip by you at home. That is something we always stress about our European Cup games at Tannadice — just as we stress the need to score away from home whenever we are on a foreign ground.

The only real worry we had heading for Spain was that our domestic performances had failed to match up to those in Europe. A draw against Forfar in the Scottish Cup was one glaring example and it bore out a long held belief of mine that no matter how well you play in Europe, and no matter how far you go, there is always the chance that a run on the Continent will cost you points in the Premier League, or find you dropping out of one of your own Cups at home. It seems to be difficult for players to keep up the same level of concentration. Of course there is scarcely any need to motivate players for matches like the Barcelona one. But it becomes very difficult to have them in the right frame of mind to play Forfar — with all due respect to them — after they have been in action against the biggest names in Europe. And when you have to journey back from a midweek game on a Thursday knowing that 48 hours later you are back in action at home there is the natural concern over how tired players can become through travelling

TOPPLING THE GIANTS

McLean shared a joke with Barcelona boss Terry Venables when the two clubs met in the UEFA Cup quarter-final clash. (Courtesy of D.C. Thomson.)

or through hanging around airports if there are delays. The glitter of Europe is fine. For us it is now essential. But behind the glamour points are lost which may at the end of the day cost a team the title!

Our displays had dipped and I had to warn the players — these same heroes from the first game — that they could be dropped. To flop against Forfar and Clydebank wasn't good enough and that had to be spelled out to them. I'm glad to say that they responded and while the score line shows that we left it late before making the break which carried us into the last four of the tournament it was a disciplined performance which delighted me. They did score in the 40th minute when Caldere struck a shot past Billy Thomson after a deflection had deceived him. But in the closing five minutes we scored twice. All the preaching of patience in Europe worked for us, as did the attitude of the fans in the half-empty stadium. The atmosphere, almost ghost-like in that huge arena, suited us. The hostile atmosphere we had been promised was not in evidence. The only cushions thrown came from their supporters at the end of the match. By then we couldn't have cared for by then we had won. Goals from John Clark and Iain Ferguson killed off the Spaniards before we had to face extra time.

It was an emotional ending and an emotional night for all of us. Even though my coach Gordon Wallace and myself had had that little bit of belief that we could go through it was still special to be able to do it with a double win over one of the most feared teams in Europe. It was a very important win for us, as I pointed out before. This was the one which put the club on the map — and had Terry Venables tipping us the following day to win the trophy.

All of it pleased me but it was specially good to see the long-serving players taste the tributes which poured in on the team, good to see them getting the praise they deserved to get and had maybe missed out on because of playing and staying loyal to an unfashionable club. Good, as well, to see someone like Jim McInally blossom in a game such as that. It became a standing joke with the players that I praised McInally so much when I'm not usually noted for sending compliments flying around the dressing room. But he was in his first season and he played magnificently for us in Europe and at home. He was another player who had been with bigger clubs — Celtic and Notts Forest — but had missed out on some of the glamour which other players there had enjoyed. These are the little things which are important even in the middle of a European triumph for the club.

And it was a triumph. It was enjoyable, even for a perfectionist like myself! In a sense it was particularly satisfying for me and for the whole club because of the difficulties which struck us during the season. They began when Davie Dodds left us to go to Switzerland and told everyone at the club the kind of deal he was getting from Neuchatel. That had a really disruptive effect on the team. Then we had Richard Gough insisting that he be sold to Spurs even though he had years of his contract still remaining. All of which shook the club to its foundations. For a spell I worried about whether everything we had built up, all the good things we had done, all the good habits which had been taught to players, would go for nothing.

Honestly, it was a crisis for this club. Some of the players who were remaining were clearly upset that a player like Dodds who was of no better quality than them was walking away from the team to make huge amounts abroad. They had a right to be upset but they take great credit from the fact that their distress didn't linger too long. Financially we tried to do something for the exceptional players, and for those players who had stayed loyal when they might have been tempted by the same kind of opportunity which took Dodds away and then also took Gough to London. Indeed, we did everything that we could for these players. The directors were very fair to them. In return the players were fair to the board and that's why having such a splendid result was a fitting

Maurice Malpas salutes an Iain Ferguson goal against Borussia Moenchengladbach at Tannadice — but the West Germans escaped when it was disallowed.

reward for the club and for the players who had remained at Tannadice no matter what kind of offer might come their way. Coming as they did, the Barcelona results were a magnificent bonus for everyone connected with Dundee United.

To go even further was still another huge boost for us all. Yet when we drew Borussia Moenchengladbach I feared trouble in the two ties. Rangers had played them earlier in the tournament and had been very unlucky to go out on the away goals rule. They had also survived a little bit of a rough house in West Germany where the second leg was played. I wanted to avoid that. I didn't want any kind of the bad feelings from that game to spill over into our own clash. So I spoke to the players beforehand and ordered them not to get involved in any on-field trouble, not simply because we wanted to have a showpiece game for a European semi-final but also for the much more important reason that we would have suffered more if we were drawn into a kicking match. It's not the way we ever play and it also upsets a team's rhythm. There is nothing worse than playing in a European match where the opposition give away foul after foul because they don't want the match to flow. We have all seen that happen and there was no way I wanted to see that at Tannadice in the first leg. I wanted an open game, a game where we

JOUSTING WITH GIANTS

The start of the move as Ferguson strikes the ball past the keeper — but Malpas does look as if he has strayed offside.

could play the football we liked to play, and a game where we would have the chance to string passes together.

My fears on that score were groundless. There was no hangover from the Rangers' game and no propaganda about trouble caused by Scots teams. Only a worry in their camp that they had lost 5-0 at Tannadice a few years earlier when their current coach Jupp Heynckes had played and now they dreaded a return to a ground with unhappy memories. But they arrived as organised and as efficient as you would expect a top-class team from the Bundesliga to be. They wanted to do to us what they had done to Rangers at Ibrox, pull us forward and then hit us on the break, and even though that had been a theme of any prematch talks we were almost caught twice as they looked for a goal in the first half.

We survived. Somewhat luckily, I admit. Then we managed to make headway in the second half and had two "goals" refused by the Belgian

TOPPLING THE GIANTS

Ian Redford tries to find a way past the so organised West Germans from Borussia in the UEFA Cup semi-final first leg.

referee after Iain Ferguson had twice put the ball past the Borussia 'keeper. Then at the death Ian Redford struck a shot which rapped against a post and the glory night we had been looking for did not materialise. But the one major factor we knew we could build upon was the fact that we had denied them an away goal. In their own Boekelberg Stadium they would have to come out, they would have to carry the game to us because, unlike the time they played Rangers, they were not in command of the situation. Then they had scored at Ibrox and with a 1-1 result there knew they were through if they held the game at 0-0. That's what they did — but now that option was not open to them. It was a situation we wanted to exploit as much as we could because we knew that Borussia were not a team who were geared to all-out attacking. They wanted to play a cat-and-mouse game and we could afford to do the same. It was a challenge we looked forward to, and a challenge the players were quick to pick up when we reached West Germany and knew that a place in the final was almost within our grasp.

Perhaps there was not the same glamour attached to Borussia as to Barcelona — in fact there was *not* the same kind of aura about them. But the performance that night in the Boekelberg ground gave me as much satisfaction as the display the players gave in the Nou Camp. Remember, this was a semi-final and we were poised to become the first Scottish team to reach the final of the UEFA Cup. To achieve such a first was very important to me and to the players. Getting the victory in West Germany brought us as much satisfaction as the possibly more acclaimed win in Spain.

I think we were helped because Jupp Heynckes underestimated us. He was convinced that he would take his team to the final — but we had other ideas. We knew we had to play them at their own game and I think the Germans felt we could not do that. Instead, it was a game which suited us. All the preaching about patience I had done down through the years in Europe paid off for us again. When Iain Ferguson scored with a diving header just before half-time I knew we had done enough to win the game. I could not see them coming back. And as the second half wore on they ran out of ideas and inspiration even though they had their best player, Uwe Rahn, the man whose goal had knocked out Rangers, back for this second-leg clash.

I worried more about the Portuguese referee than I worried about Rahn or any of the other Borussia players. I was convinced that Senor Rosa Dos Santos would award a crucial decision against us. He was under pressure from the bulk of the crowd, under pressure from the German players and we had suffered in the past from referees bending over backwards to help home teams. It's an accepted part of the European tournaments and as time ran out I felt sure that he would award a penalty against us. He didn't do that but he did give a bizarre decision against Billy Thomson which led to them having their most threatening moment of the match when Borowka thumped a shot against the post. At the end, though, they didn't get any more breaks from the referee and we were the team to score in the last minute when Ian Redford sent the ball past Uwe Kamps in the Borussia goal.

It's hard to describe how we all felt that night. There we were in a European final, a little team half of Europe had never heard of when

Jim McInally moves in to tackle a Borussia player in the Tannadice match between the two teams.

the season started. I believe that I took more satisfaction from our run in Europe than I took when we won the Premier League. As I pointed out earlier, we had lost key men at the club, yet somehow we had still reached this European summit. It was all a little hard to believe.

Of course, I couldn't be completely happy about things — the perfectionist in me has to pop out all the time. I didn't like the fact that so many of the team who had reached the UEFA final — and the Scottish Cup final too — had been bought in the transfer market. Only four of the players who played from the start in Moenchengladbach were home-grown talent — Dave Narey, Billy Kirkwood, Paul Sturrock and John Holt. Yet, basically, I still cling to my early belief when I took over at Tannadice, that we are a club who must breed our own players. That upset me.

It's the morning after and United stars Jim McInally, man of the match, and goal scorer Kevin Gallacher share a bath at Tannadice as the realisation soaks in that they have beaten Barcelona.

Not that it had cost the club money. All the players who had joined us from other clubs had been paid for by outgoing transfers. We were still balancing the books — indeed, more than just balancing the books. At that time we had around a million pounds in the bank and the club was in the healthiest position it had ever been in. But it is hard for me to alter my thinking. In our early years I concentrated on developing our own youth policy and at one stage we had three-quarters of the team who were local. That has changed but I still see the future of Dundee United as a club bringing youngsters through the system rather than a club buying success through the transfer market. We were forced to do that, forced into making buys because we had lost experienced players and had to replace them with experienced men. You cannot compete in the Premier League with a team of youngsters. That is just not possible. In fact the League set-up holds back the progress of younger players and so you have to become involved in the transfer market. We have been lucky because we have mostly been able to get the right type of player here. That is important. One bad hat in the dressing-room can ruin a club.

The team we have now is not as good a team in some respects as the title-winning side. We don't have the same high skill factor as we had before in some areas of the team. Yet they make up for that by being able to battle when the going gets tough and by showing tremendous determination — and that is an ingredient we were accused of lacking in the past. So you get a balance — a loss on one hand but a gain on the other, and with the problems we faced last season grit and determination were what we needed most of all! That's what took us to the final of the UEFA Cup against IFK Gothenburg and almost won us the trophy.

Chapter Five

SO CLOSE TO GLORY IN GOTHENBURG

Going to Gothenburg to play in the final of the UEFA Cup was one of the highlights of my entire career. In its own way it rivalled the winning of the two League Cups and even the Premier League triumph at home. All of them meant a great deal to me and to the club. But Europe has that special lure about it, that extra bit of glamour, that hint of immortality if you can achieve success in one of the Continent's top competitions.

We were the first Scottish team to play in the final of that particular tournament. That in itself brought the club some distinction, but we all desperately wanted to become only the fourth Scottish club in history to win a European cup. Celtic under Jock Stein had taken the biggest prize of all when they won the European Cup in 1967. Five years later Rangers under Willie Waddell went to Barcelona to win the European Cup Winners Cup. And then, in 1983, my north-east rival Alex Ferguson took Aberdeen to a victory over Real Madrid in that same competition. That game was played on the same Ullevi Stadium where we were playing our first-leg match against IFK Gothenburg. When we were heading home from Moenchengladbach that seemed as if it might be a lucky omen for us. Aberdeen had gone there to win — if we could repeat that performance and then have a second leg at home the Cup could be sitting in the Tannadice board room. Ironically the

A dream has died but Jim McLean still goes out onto the Tannadice pitch to salute the Dundee United supporters after the defeat from Gothenburg in the final of the UEFA Cup. (Courtesy of D.C. Thomson.)

stadium, built for the World Cup finals in 1958, was to become our biggest problem!

In saying that I'm not attempting in any way to run down the Swedish team. Nor am I trying to suggest that their coach Gunder Bengtsson didn't impress me. He did, and so did the Gothenburg team. But the playing surface at the Ullevi was always going to be as big a danger to our chances of winning as anything the Swedish team could do against us. I knew that the first moment I set eyes on it. My assistant Gordon Wallace and myself went to see them play in a Swedish First Division game. We knew they would be impressive, and they were. We knew they would be well organised, and they were. We knew they had unearthed a new strike force who would be dangerous, and they were.

While all of these things registered, though, it was the state of the pitch which constantly invaded my thoughts. So much so that both Gordon and I agreed that publicly we had to play down the problems that the bumpy, rutted, uneven pitch would bring us. Even in the privacy of the dressing-room we decided that it would be wrong to tell the players too much about the playing surface. Really it was a disgrace. No cup final should ever have been played on that pitch. Don't think I'm making excuses — I'm not doing that. It is a fact that the pitch was bad and anyone there would tell you the same. It was very badly rutted and that created a massive problem for us.

All my managerial career I had been preaching the same message to the players. I had always stressed that when you had possession of the ball it was essential that you kept it, that you made it very, very difficult for the opposing team to take it away from you. That meant a style based on close passing, a style where you kept the ball at all costs. If that meant passing it around in the back four, especially away from home in Europe, then that's what you did. It was a style which had worked for us in Europe, a style which had helped get us the successes we had enjoyed before that memorable season which climaxed on one of the worst pitches we have ever been asked to play on. Initially we steered clear of the subject. Then once the players had seen the ground we knew that we had to try to tell them to change their normal game. There could be no square passing. There could be no short passing. There could be no back passing. None of these could be employed in this game because on the surface of the Ullevi Stadium the ball was going to stick. Passes would be held up or would go astray because of the ruts and bumps which scarred the pitch. We could not risk that happening around our defensive area. So suddenly we were telling them they had

SO CLOSE TO GLORY IN GOTHENBURG

An angry moment as John Clark faces up to four Swedish stars in the UEFA final against Gothenburg in Dundee.

to play a long-ball game, something totally foreign to their nature and something they cannot do effectively. Everything we had taught them, all the hours and the days, the weeks and the months, and even the years of hammering out a message on training grounds, had gone to waste.

We toiled badly and while that was due to a difficulty the players had in adapting to a different approach there were also psychological problems once they realised how bad the pitch was going to be. Neither Gordon nor myself had mentioned it, but rumours had filtered through to the players about the playing conditions they were going to face. Then when they arrived for training they saw for themselves. It affected their confidence. There is no doubt in my mind about that. I knew that it would and I knew that I would find that hard to handle in the preparations for the first leg.

The psychological problems which seem to afflict the modern player have always been difficult for me. As a tactical manager I would expect reasonable marks out of ten from anyone because I feel that I have proved myself there. On the mental side, on being able to talk players out of whatever problems they imagine they might have, then I would score low marks. I cannot seem to get on the proper wavelength with them. I find it impossible to sort out players' heads. So I knew that the shock of seeing the Ullevi pitch would present us with all kinds of worries.

Sometimes I feel that players need a psychologist rather than a manager. I have told some of them that. You would not believe some of the ideas which become implanted in the minds of players. I can go back to the time I was starting out as manager here at Tannadice and one of the players, Tommy Traynor, came to me and explained that I shouldn't look for too many good performances from him after we had played maybe 14 or 15 games. "I go off form every season around that time," he told me. He was quite serious too and he obviously believed this even though there was no reason for it to happen. Anyhow, the next season after a game at Kilmarnock when we had been down 2-0 and ended up winning 3-2 the same player again came to speak to me after the match. He had not been in the team and this was about the sixth game of the season. He told me: "When I went on as a substitute today I felt good, better than at any other time this season. You have to remember that I'm a slow starter." I couldn't believe my ears. I said to him then, "Do you remember what you told me last season? You went off form after 14 games. Now you don't start until the sixth or seventh match. So you're going to be good for half a dozen games every year."

Yet Tommy Traynor believed that and I'm left with the job of trying to convince him that he is wrong. How do you do it? After 16 years as manager I don't think I'm very much closer to finding out the answer.

Even in the season following the World Cup in Mexico I had to try to deal with a constant problem from one of our more experienced players, Eamonn Bannon — one of the men we would have been relying on in a season where the demands were even greater than they had ever been before. Eamonn had got it into his head that he had to change his style of play. He was completely convinced about this and I spent the whole season trying to tell him how wrong he was.

I know he won't agree with what I'm saying here — he didn't agree during the season so it's doubtful if he would change his mind now! First of all he complained that he was tired after being in Mexico with

SO CLOSE TO GLORY IN GOTHENBURG

Striker Kevin Gallacher moves beyond the Gothenburg defence to get in a shot — but his luck was out.

Scotland. Then he also decided that the way he had been playing for the past ten years was wrong for him now. Since that had got into his mind his form deteriorated badly. He stopped doing what he is best at. Eamonn Bannon is an exciting player when he plays the way he has played for us since coming back from Chelsea, attacking defenders and then getting crosses into the penalty box. It is the hardest thing in the game to do and yet he did it for us for a long time. Season after season he won us games by playing that way. Then suddenly after playing in the World Cup finals he decided that he cannot do it any longer.

Why? I don't know. It can't be his age. He is only 28. If he had been five years older then I might have been able to look at the situation with some understanding. But he has made up his mind that he cannot run the way he did before. In one sense I agreed — he could not go up and down the field in the same way and so I asked him to stay further upfield instead of dropping so deep he is practically standing on

Maurice Malpas's toes. But that is just one small point. Basically he has decided he wants to become a passer of the ball — and that is not his game. He cannot play that way. But for whatever reason he wants to abandon what he is good at and try an approach which will make him less effective as a player. Because of all this Eamonn Bannon put in a whole season — and a very long season at that — where he showed only indifferent form. All because mentally he believes that he cannot make the same contribution physically as he has done in all the other years. To me that will happen when he is in his mid-thirties, but it isn't going to happen now. To think that way is ridiculous.

The kind of thinking which produces that kind of form crisis angers me. Maybe I should be better equipped now to take something like that in my stride. But I can't. It infuriates me and I frankly admit that it all becomes too much for me to try to solve problems of that nature. More and more it appears to become an increasing part of a manager's job — but I don't see why it should be! Refusing to accept psychological problem-solving as a genuine part of my job means worries for me at certain times. Gothenburg was one of them and I did not tackle that pitch problem the way I should have been able to do. I worried enough over the change in tactics which was being forced upon the team. Basically I didn't want to make too great an issue of the Ullevi pitch and then allow the players to have a ready-made excuse if things went wrong. It would have been too easy for them to hang their hats on that as a major excuse — I wanted to avoid that at all costs.

The basic worry for us was that we are at our best on a good playing surface. I can remember going to play PSV Eindhoven in Holland and from the moment the players saw the pitch I knew that we were going to win the game. In Barcelona the surface was absolutely perfect and as a bonus the Spaniards watered it and that made it even better for us. At Moenchengladbach the Boekelberg Stadium was excellent. It was only in the final that we encountered problems and we found it difficult to cope with them.

In one sense, of course, the season was also beginning to catch up on us by that stage. The number of matches our key players had been asked to play was into the seventies and so many of these had been vital, either in the various cup competitions or in the cut-throat atmosphere of the Premier League. From Barcelona onwards the energy had started to drain from us. There are only so many times you can ask a team to peak in any one season. Only so many times you can demand extra effort from players who have had too many demands placed on

SO CLOSE TO GLORY IN GOTHENBURG

The Gothenburg keeper touches this try over the bar as Iain Ferguson, kneeling, watches.

them already. We found that out the hard way.

Ian Redford hit it all on the head for us when we eventually discussed what finally went wrong for us in the closing stages of the season. He pointed out that he did not feel any real difficulty physically as far as the demands being made on all of the players were concerned but he reckoned that mentally we could not peak as often as we had to. From March onwards we were making constant demands on our player pool. It's almost as if Europe becomes a two-stage situation. You have one part of the tournament before Christmas and then the second part from March onwards. We handled the first part OK with our wins over Lens and Craiova and Hajduk Split being put together over a four-month period. But the three months where we had to finish off the tournament, plus challenge in the Premier League and in the Scottish Cup, placed enormous pressure on everyone connected with the club.

Barcelona was a major game. As well as being a European quarter-final, we were paired with one of the Continent's greatest clubs. When it came to playing the West Germans, Borussia Moenchengladbach, the tie may have lacked some of the glitter which attached itself to Barcelona and their host of stars but it was a two-legged semi-final. That alone made it certain that the extra efforts required from the players would be greater than normal. Any semi-final is a gruelling experience: in Europe the tension which is always there doubles. Over the two legs the intensity is enormous. Then, of course, we had the two legs of the final, while, at home, we had to face Dundee in a Scottish Cup semi-final at Tynecastle and then after winning that difficult derby game had to face St Mirren in the final!

It was the kind of programme which would have broken bigger clubs than Dundee United. Somehow we kept going until the last fatal days of the season. How we did it I don't know. What I do know is that when it came to the second leg against the Swedes some of the players were out on their feet, and as well as the constant pressures, they had to come to terms with losing in the Scottish Cup final just a few days earlier.

It was not exactly the best preparation. Everyone in Scotland remembered what had happened to poor Hearts just a year earlier. They had lost in the Premier League to Dundee at Dens Park on the last day of the season — a result which gave Celtic the title. Then a week later they had gone down to Aberdeen in the Scottish Cup final. Inside a week a team which had been chasing a double had finished with nothing. That thought was in all our minds, too, as we approached the Gothenburg games. There were other problems for us, of course. The Swedish season was just getting under way and their players were fresher than we were. They had had the benefit of a winter break and somehow, quite mistakenly in my view, people did not rate them as highly as they had rated either of our opponents in the two previous rounds.

I rated them highly. Before I watched them with Gordon Wallace on our spy trip I had known about their players and their style. A year earlier they had beaten Aberdeen on the away goals rule in the quarter-final of the European Cup. Then Alex Ferguson had praised them highly and eventually tried to buy their striker, Johnny Ekstroem, who moved to Italy for a large fee. Since his departure and the retiral of Torben Nilsson, Gothenburg had brought together a new, equally deadly, strike force. Lennart Nilsson had been bought from another Swedish club and Stefan Petterson had been pushed up front from the midfield role he had held against Aberdeen. Their coach Gunder

SO CLOSE TO GLORY IN GOTHENBURG

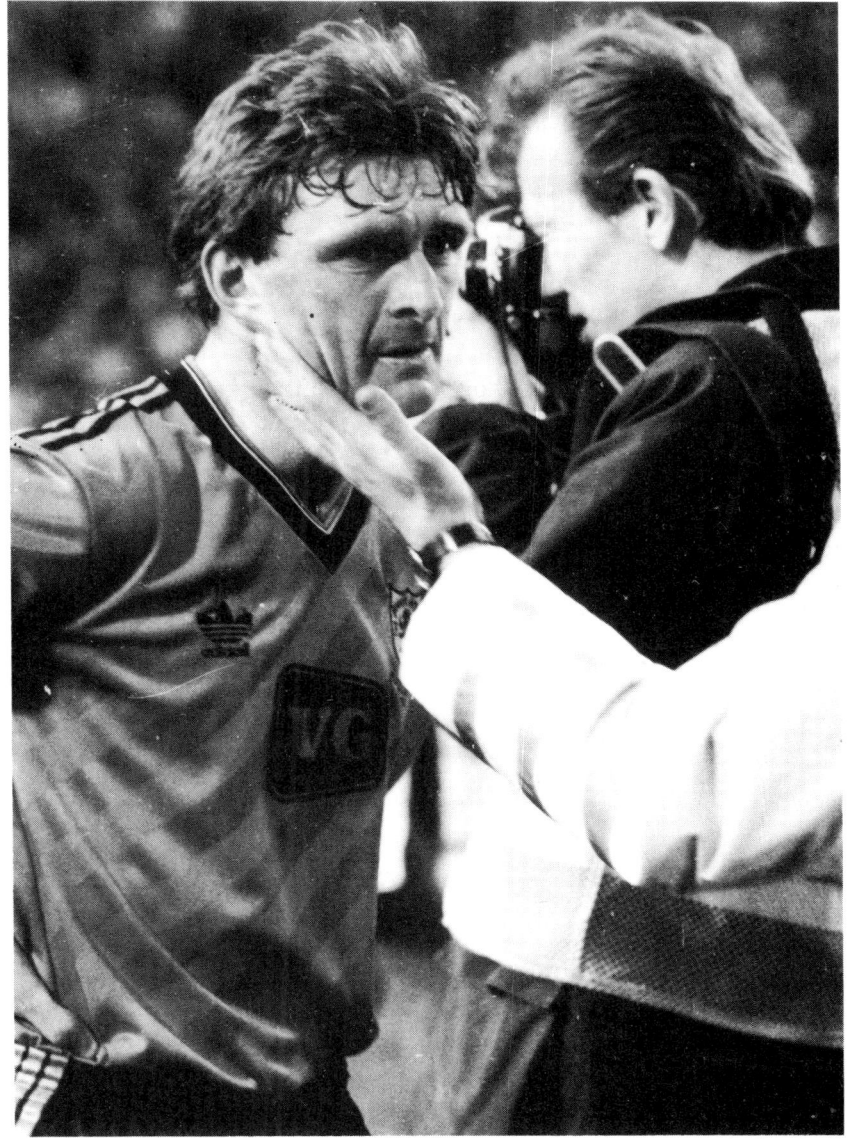

The dream is over and all the agony felt by the Dundee United players is etched in Paul Hegarty's face at the end of the second leg of the UEFA Cup final against Gothenburg.

Bengtsson had exactly the right blend in the front men. He had Petterson, who would take the ball to feet and then move in on goal, and he had Nilsson, who would make runs in behind the defence. It was a brilliant partnership and we knew that from the first time we saw them play together. At the back they had another excellent partnership at the heart of the defence. The two central defenders, Glenn Hysen and Peter Larsson, were very, very good in my opinion.

Their players had a lot to play for too. As well as the obvious glory which comes from winning a European trophy, the Swedish part-timers had their eyes fixed on transfers which would make them very rich. Hysen was one who moved on but at that time others were being watched by the top Italian clubs and I realised that in the first leg in particular on their own ground they would be raising their game even higher than normal as they aimed for a massive lira-laden pay day.

I quite honestly rated their two front men as a better pairing than Mark Hughes and Gary Lineker. Their reputations were not as great, their names not as well known, but their uncanny understanding and their ability to complement one another made them much more dangerous to us than the Barcelona big names. Most of all, though, I rated Gothenberg as a more formidable team than either of the big-name sides we had beaten. They were magnificently organised. In fact their system never altered and within that way of playing few teams in Europe would be any better. I doubt if I have seen any team who would be able to match them for the discipline and organisation they showed within that framework devised by their coach. It was the part of their play I admired more than any other. I could look at the central defenders and rate them highly; I could envy them the two strikers and the menace they caused; but most of all it was the playing system which impressed me.

Gothenburg did not have players with massive reputations. In that respect they could not match the big stars who had been paraded by Barcelona in our two ties against them, or even rival the more modest but still highly acclaimed West Germans from Borussia. As a team, however, they were better than either of these two sides. The 4-4-2 set-up they favoured suited the players they had and suited the patient way they liked to play. It's a pattern which I admire, but it's not always possible for a Scottish team to use it. As well as patience from the players you need patience from the support. Not all of our fans would stand for the slower, more methodical, build-up. Our fans, and I mean by that the Scottish fan in general, want the ball played forward far too early. They want to get it up there in the opposition half as quickly as possible. That is not always the best way to approach the game.

Ace Gothenburg striker Stefan Pettersen is closely marked by World Cup men Dave Narey and Maurice Malpas.

JOUSTING WITH GIANTS

Certainly in Europe it's usually the wrong way to go about things because it's then when you hurl people forward that you are caught with the kind of counter-attacks teams like Gothenburg have mastered. It's the way we would always like to play but we don't always find possible to do so. It's a way we would have wanted to play if the Ullevi Stadium pitch had matched the perfect turf of the Nou Camp Stadium in Barcelona. But while the Swedes were used to the dreadful surface we had to try to pick our way through what became a soccer minefield packed with potential match-losing mistakes.

It was a major handicap to us not being able to sit back and play the possession football which would have sucked them forward and allowed us space to play in their half of the field. It had worked so well in the earlier rounds but now it wasn't possible. We had to try to change things to play the way Scottish fans like to see the games played. It was not a game which had us feeling comfortable. We were looking to play the way Liverpool play, or the way the old Leeds United team with Johnny Giles and Billy Bremner and the others played. It is hard enough to do that at the best of times because while fans like to see Continental or South American teams doing it, they don't enjoy their own teams employing the same patient passing game.

Gothenburg could use it and their fans would expect it. They played their passes more or less as they always did. They played with the kind of composure which had taken them to the semi-final of the European Cup a year earlier, with the same patience and skill which had brought them a quarter-final victory over the redoubtable Italians, Inter Milan. As we approached the final it was too often overlooked that Gothenburg had gone to the San Siro Stadium and in front of more than 60,000 fans had beaten Inter 1-0. It ranked with our display in Barcelona and acted as a warning to myself and to my players.

But all the warnings were not enough to give us even the draw which would have satisfied me in that first-leg game. I went into the match looking and hoping for the kind of away form we had shown in the two previous rounds. Remember, wins away from home had guaranteed us our place in the final . . . we would have liked a repeat. Yet, knowing how superbly drilled the Swedes were, I recognised deep down that I would have happily settled for a draw before the kick off. On the night, though, with thousands of our own supporters among the 50,000 gate, even a draw was beyond us.

A combination of circumstances brought the Swedes the goal which was to give them victory in that important first-leg game. Ironically the

SO CLOSE TO GLORY IN GOTHENBURG

Another close thing against Gothenburg — but not close enough for striker Iain Ferguson to get the goal he wanted.

pitch we had dreaded so much helped cost us the goal seven minutes before half time. They took a corner on the left and as we tried to mark their giant defender, Glenn Hysen, Petterson sneaked in to send a header towards goal. It bounced and reared up from one of the bumps in the pitch to deceive Billy Thomson. It was a crazy moment as the freak bounce took the ball into goal. We were not helped by the fact that Thomson had been injured earlier in the game after he had dived at Nilsson's feet in the opening minutes of the game. It was a brave dive by Billy but it brought him five *double* stitches and left him still dazed at the time they snatched that solitary goal of the night. After that he recovered to make several fine stops but there is no doubt that his judgment was still impaired when Gothenburg scored.

There was little point in dwelling on that. We had failed to get an away goal, but we had managed to keep Gothenburg to just one goal on a pitch which had caused us nightmares. To some extent the psychological balance that night after the game tilted a little towards us. Their coach Gunder Bengtsson admitted that his team were going to be facing the "hardest game of the tournament so far" when they came to Tannadice in two weeks' time. Their goalscorer Stefan Petterson declared that one goal would not be enough to give them the trophy they had won five years earlier. He insisted that they would have to score another goal if they were to clinch a victory. All of that was encouraging, but then we did not know what was ahead of us. We did realise that we faced the Scottish Cup final against St Mirren four days before the return. What none of us could know was that we were to lose to the Paisley team and just how much that defeat would drain the last ounces of courage and determination from a team who had met so many demands on so many different occasions in a season which had been harder on the side than any other in all my years in charge. Basically we were asking for far too much from far too few. At a club like Dundee United where you are limited in the number of quality players you have it is essential that you have almost all of your players reaching their full potential during each big game. If you drop below that then you are going to suffer the kind of defeat which waited for us against Gothenburg. Some of the players were practically out on their feet. They were drained both physically and mentally. Our players were asked to peak too often in too short a time. If we had more players available, a stronger pool of players for first-team duty, then it might have helped. But we might have finished up with the same problem if the players we had did not come up to the high standard you need for an assault on Europe. We were not able to scale the same heights in the two Gothenburg games as we had in the earlier rounds of the competition.

I believe that if you have exceptional players then they can drop a little from their best and still be good enough to get a result. Our problem has always been that we have never had enough of these exceptional players. Don't get me wrong, I'm not trying to malign the players we have had at Tannadice. I'm simply pointing out facts. At any given time in the 16 years I have been manager we have never had more than six really top-class players in the team. Therefore we have always needed to have nine players playing to their absolute best to give us the outstanding results we have managed to achieve.

Basically we have sometimes been caught dreaming about how well we might have done if we had Andy Gray or Raymond Stewart still around in the team. If it had been possible to hold on to all of the players then we would have had that many more class footballers in the side. But it would have been a disastrous course financially for this club to take that road. We had to sell to be able to survive alongside the top teams in Scotland who have a better power base in terms of support than we do.

Going back to the second leg at Tannadice, it was always going to be that game too many. Beforehand I tried to lift the players. We had let down our supporters at Hampden against St Mirren in the Cup final a few days earlier and I wanted them fired up and angry enough to shake off their exhaustion and make a comeback to form against Gothenburg. Personally I felt I had let the fans down by some of the decisions I made before and during the Scottish Cup final. Also, though, the players did not give the kind of performance the fans deserved to see from them. So I wanted them to go out on their own ground and show the whole of Europe that they were good enough to win the UEFA Cup. It didn't work out that way. Again we saw luck turn cruelly against us during the match. We wanted to turn the game into an old-fashioned Scottish Cup tie and force Gothenburg to abandon their carefully cultivated system of playing. But when they scored in 22 minutes I think we all knew the task was going to be too much for the players.

Yet, while we had had breaks earlier in the competition, as so often happens we had none when we needed them most of all. One little twist of fate going our way might just have given the players that little bit of inspiration they needed so badly. It did not come — at least not for us. Instead it went to the Swedes when Tord Holmgren sent Paul Sturrock crashing to the ground before hoisting a long through ball into our half of the field. Sturrock was left sprawling as the Rumanian referee waved play on. The crowd roared for a free kick, nothing was given and Lennart Nilsson, one of their danger men, went past a challenge from John Clark and hammered a shot past Billy Thomson from 25 yards.

Now we needed three goals if we were to win the final. That away goal coming so early and coming the way that it did was a killer blow. When Iain Ferguson hit the bar with a header before half time I think we all knew that it was not our night. That it was not our year! We did score with a John Clark shot after an hour but to be absolutely honest Gothenburg were the better team over the two legs. My players gave me everything they had left but that wasn't enough for what we had to ask them to do. Gothenburg were too strong for us to combat with the little we had in reserve.

As I said earlier, their strengths were their central defenders and their two front men — allied of course to their playing system. Ironically, that was always where we had had our own strengths. In the past we had Paul Hegarty and Dave Narey at their best and then we had

Paul Sturrock and Davie Dodds playing together up front. If we had had these combinations then we might have had the win we wanted so much. Their players came closer, too, to reaching the higher levels of performance which are needed by winners. We couldn't do that all over again and deep in my heart I know that I'll probably never have the chance of winning a European trophy again. You know, that night at Tannadice I never once looked at the UEFA Cup. To this day I've never seen it, except in photographs. I didn't go to look at it and I didn't touch it because for some reason I thought it would bring us bad luck. I wish now I had touched it because that's the closest I'll ever be to a European cup. In the end all the little superstitious things made no difference. We lost and the players were in tears and the fans who had followed us so loyally had to watch as we finished a memorable season without a trophy to show for all the effort which had been put in.

But, just taking part in that final will live on in my memory for as long as I live. It was an occasion which brought credit to the club and the fans and recognition to the players. So if the memory is tinged with an understandable amount of sadness it is also coloured with a pride in the supporters. I think that our fans showed the world that football is not only about winners. Sure, in the game we tend to be judged on what we have won and at the end of that season we had won nothing. Yet as far as the fans were concerned they had seen us reach heights we had never reached before. They had seen us beat Barcelona and Borussia. They had seen us as the first Scottish team to play in the final of the UEFA Cup. And they stayed on the terracings to salute us and to salute Gothenburg as well.

Maybe we had not won anything — but the fans were winners in my book. They stayed there that night long after the game until I went out to wave to them. It means a great deal to me. At a time in the game when English clubs remain banned because of the Heysel Stadium disaster and when crowd troubles so often capture the headlines across the Continent our supporters gave us all a night to remember with happiness. They helped put a smile back on the face of the game. Millions of people in 19 different countries looked in on television and they saw a final played the way finals should always be played. They saw a sporting game on the field and they saw sportsmanship on the terracings. Just as our fans had been welcomed in Gothenburg, so their fans were welcomed to our city. It made me feel very proud on a night which probably brought me the worst moments of my career.

There is no way you can put into words the emptiness you feel after

On the way to Gothenburg and Paul Sturrock heads for the charter jet followed by World Cup mate Maurice Malpas.

JOUSTING WITH GIANTS

an important result goes against you. This one was worse than any other because it was the second final we had lost in the space of four days. Watching players in tears after that Gothenburg game brought it home to me just how much they had all given during the season. It may not have brought us victory but I like to think that it was a season which put the club on the map and which must have enhanced the standing of the club all across the world.

Losers are often forgotten. That is a sad yet cruel fact of football life. But I don't think we will fade away from people's minds too easily. They will remember those earlier jousts with the giants when we won and they will remember how a little club could still show Europe how to handle defeat no matter how bitter that might be. Professionally it was a black, bleak night for me — emotionally, at the end, I realised there was more to football than simply winning. Our supporters showed me that.

Chapter Six

POPULARITY IS OUT

My type of football management is not right for everyone — but most emphatically it is right for me. There is no way I could do the job without having the single-minded approach which has brought me any success I have had so far. It hasn't won me any popularity contests with the players but it's not designed to do that. It's designed to get the best possible performances from the players for Dundee United Football Club.

It's true that I would have liked to be more popular with the players. It would have been good to have the kind of easy-going relationship with the lads at Tannadice as I had with the players at Dens Park when I was a coach there. It was not possible. As a coach you could mix more with the players, relax with them, joke with them because any cruel decision which might affect them would be made by the manager. That was where the buck stopped. At Tannadice it has always stopped with me and I realised from the very beginning that it was not my job to seek popularity with the players. If a manager is liked by the players then you can look for him being out of a job very quickly. He will get the sack because the players will eventually let him down. It's human nature, again. If players get it easy in training then they'll take it easy in games, and if that is all happening because the manager has been taking it easy too then he is the one who loses his job. Players won't give their best unless they are pushed. I firmly believe that. The game has been littered with managerial victims who have been sacked by clubs because they were not hard enough on the players. There are far too many really nice fellows who are out of a job because they have not been hard enough.

I remember back in the early days as a manager here I was coming back on the team bus from a match against St Mirren at Paisley. I must have given one of my better dressing-room performances after it because on the journey to Dundee Doug Cowie, who was a member of the backroom staff, asked me, "Do you not think you are too hard on the players?" I told Dougie then: "No. I know that I am hard on them, that I demand a lot from them but if I'm going to be a good manager then I will have to be hard on them. If I have to be a b . . . . . . to them then that's exactly what I'll be. It may be the only chance I have of being a good manager. And of being successful."

When I first came into the job that was the basis of many of my thoughts. I felt that if I was going to get the sack — and that is a probability that most managers have to face up to — then I would get it because the players had not done what I wanted them to do. I made it clear to all the players that they would know exactly what I was looking for from each one of them before the game. Similarly, after the game they would be told exactly what I had thought of their performances. As far as I'm concerned there is no hiding place in that dressing-room. Players can hide on the field. Hide in the sense that they won't want passes from team mates because they are playing badly. Or hide in the sense that they will not look honestly at their own performance but try to pass the buck to others. It's always been my theory that in a team game a player can duck out of responsibility too easily. In a way it's easier for a person to be dishonest in a team game whereas it's impossible for that to happen in an individual sport. Golfers and tennis players don't have the same attitude as footballers. In our game players want to look around at others. They want to look sideways or look over their shoulders or look up front at the other players in the team. Then they can convince themselves that their very ordinary performance in the game has become that wee bit better in comparison with someone else in the team. All the time I've been in the game as player and as a manager that has happened. It's wrong. Players still do it today just as they did when I was playing. I've done it myself. I've taken that look around me and then decided that someone else was worse than me, so I'm OK. It's not as easy as that. All you are doing there is cheating

POPULARITY IS OUT

The brothers McLean — Tommy, now boss of Motherwell, Jim and Willie, who also managed Motherwell but is now out of football. (Courtesy of D.C. Thomson.)

yourself and cheating your team mates. You are selling everyone short. The only thing that should be important is how you played yourself. If you are not good enough then you have to own up to that instead of sliding off looking for excuses. Or trying to blame someone else in the team for the problems. In the end it doesn't work. If you adopt a philosophy that is going to bring in other players all the time then it is a false philosophy because eventually you will become the kind of player who refuses to accept any kind of responsibility. I have never accepted this attitude since becoming a manager. Apparently at Aberdeen their goalkeeper Bobby Clark held firmly to a theory that if he lost a goal then he had to blame someone else. And do it quickly. That way the blame didn't reach him. When we signed John Gardiner, the reserve from

Pittodrie, he arrived at Tannadice with that scenario firmly in his mind. It was never going to be his fault. I have no time for that kind of thinking.

I stand by my decisions and players should stand by their own actions. When I came in the door here I stressed that I would stand or fall by my *own* actions. I didn't know whether I was going to be right or wrong with so many of them — though, fortunately, I think I have been right with most of them. One of the things I promised was that every player would know exactly what I was thinking and why I might be thinking that way. Beyond any shadow of doubt any player who is here, or who has been here under my management, knows why they were left out of certain games. Or why certain tactics were used. If they play one week and are out the next then I tell them why. It may be they played badly or it may be for tactical reasons — but they are told. And they are told honestly. That is very, very important in my view. I know there are some managers who leave players out of teams without offering any explanations but it's not the way I have done things here. They are told. By me. Personally.

No one in the team is ever in any doubt as to what is expected from him. We make severe demands on players here — but no more than we make on ourselves. I know that people think it's wrong for me to criticise players and performances but I am that way because I won't do anything behind anyone's back. I tell players to their faces what I think of them and how I think they played, whether that is good or bad. I won't have it any other way. Some people outside the club — and some inside the club too — believe that I moan and groan too much, that I push too hard and make too many demands on the players. I think that's utter rubbish. Maybe there have been times when I have pulled back, times when I worried about going too far, times when I've seen players almost reduced to tears because I have been laying into them in the dressing-room. But it has been for their good and for the team's good. I never put players under any more severe scrutiny than I put myself under. They go through that in the dressing room after the game — I go through it at home that night, or even lying awake still worrying about where things might have gone wrong. Quite honestly, I have lain in bed after really disappointing results and cried because of some aspect of the game where I felt I had failed the club, failed the players and failed the supporters. I know when I've been wrong and I have suffered more than any of the players have ever suffered.

I know that the demands placed on them have been great. I know that

Jim steps into the hot seat as manager of Dundee United in December 1971. Here he is along with outgoing manager Jerry Kerr. (Courtesy of D.C. Thomson.)

the expectations I've held out for have been high. But I firmly hold to the view that if I placed them any lower then performances would have dipped. We would not have had the success we have enjoyed over the past years if I had not made demands on the squad. If I had asked for less from them, then they would have given less. Not all of them, maybe, but most of them. You have always to remember that players win games — managers lose them. The manager is just one more person for players to hide behind when things go wrong. Lawrie McMenemy said that and he was right.

I have been accused of criticising players so much that I have affected their confidence. On occasions in my drive for perfection it's possible that I have upset certain players. But the truth is that this is balanced by the times when things go well after I've said my piece. There was the time in a Cup final a few years back when I lost the head completely with Ralph Milne at half time. I admit that freely. I was ready to lynch him because he was not doing what he had been told to do. He blamed me for us losing that final to Rangers but the facts are a little bit different from the way he recalls them. It was 0-0 when they came into the dressing room at the interval. I did threaten him — and it paid off in the second half. He did what I asked him to do: he drove at the full-back, cut inside him and then hammered a left-foot shot into the net. That's what we had wanted from him in the first half and that's why I had a go at him after he had failed to do what we wanted. If he wants to deny that there was a response from him he can do so, but I know differently and so do the fans who saw the goal. My talk-in worked. Maybe he didn't like it but it brought a goal from Ralph Milne. He went on to say that I had lost them that final. But we scored again that day through Paul Sturrock and it was disallowed because John Holt was offside. How was I to blame for that?

If it had come from another of the players then I think I would have been a little bit more upset. Coming from Ralph, it was no surprise. It was the kind of thing you learned to expect from him. He was a typical example of the attitude I talked about earlier — when things went wrong Ralph would look around and blame everyone but himself. That was always his way. Everyone at the club knew that and I think maybe the fans learned to recognise it as well. They never did like him. I would doubt if there were many tears shed on the terracings when he finally left to join Charlton. He could have achieved so much more but when the big demands were made Ralph was often posted missing.

Players can win games by their performances and I see my job as

POPULARITY IS OUT

One of his rare smiles is captured here as McLean meets the Press before one of his club's major European games. (Courtesy of D.C. Thomson.)

getting the best possible performances out of players. I have to motivate them the best way that I can. Sometimes they won't like it but if the end result brings a good display from the player, gets the player to fulfil his potential, and also brings us a win as a club, then I am going to be satisfied.

There was the highly publicised time when in a game against Motherwell I was supposed to have fined the players for lack of entertainment after they had scored five goals in the first half in the Scottish Cup tie at Tannadice. Eventually we won the game 6-1 but there were times when we were sluggish, times when we might have thrown the game away and gone out of the Cup. I wasn't happy with that and I docked the players a special bonus payment which was on offer then if they produced an exceptional performance. Against smaller teams we often have them on a win bonus and this extra £50 if the display they give is a very special one. Although we won 6-1 I didn't think they merited that extra payment. It was as simple as that and I had a message to get home to them that day. I wanted them to realise that supporters come along to games to be entertained for 90 minutes — not just 45 minutes. On that day the 45 minutes was enough to give us a win and send us on our way to the final — we reached Hampden again that year. But on many occasions it would not have been enough.

The success we have had has come about because of dedication and application. Sometimes we have paid more attention to the smallest details than some of the other clubs have done. But that has been essential for us. We don't have any right to be among the best teams in the country. We have to fight hard all the time to be in there challenging for honours. Maybe we have to be that wee bit fitter, maybe that wee bit better organised than the others to make up for the things which are not available to us. We don't have the huge crowds that other teams command, we don't have the massive numbers on the terracings that the Old Firm have — and that's where the real stimulus for players comes from.

Nothing lifts players more than big crowds at games. Money doesn't give them the boost that a big match atmosphere provides. It's that whole feeling that surrounds glamour games which gets the adrenalin pumping and has players on edge. It's also in these games that you don't have to work too hard to motivate the really good players, the honest players in the team. They respond without you having to drive them too much.

I do admit to having problems with my coaching methods now because I try to dissect every player's game and diagnose their faults so thoroughly that I can inhibit them. What I have been attempting to do recently is to strike a balance in my approach to certain players. Instead of only pointing out glaring weaknesses in their play I have also been trying to encourage them to express themselves more in the things they are good at. It's always been my way to demand that players work on their weak points — that's the only way you will get real improvement in anyone's game. Now with a little more experience, and with a little more confidence in myself and my ideas, and probably more confidence in my players too, I'm ready to let them do more on their own.

There have been times recently when I've been able to look back with pride at some of the things we have done. Little matters like the way we have played in the second half of some important game. We have given better displays after the half-time team talk and so I must be doing my job properly.

POPULARITY IS OUT

If I have had to lay into players then that's just a part of my job. No one likes criticism. I don't like it myself — but on occasions it's necessary. If I were to duck out of that then I would be cheating myself and cheating my players. That would not be right. The basis of this club's success is built on honesty and loyalty. These are the twin pillars Dundee United is built on. I would not want it any other way.

Players have to recognise that any stick I hand out to them is as much for their good as for mine or the club's. Most of them do realise that and a fantastic percentage of them have appreciated it. I think players have to ask themselves if they would have been happier if I had simply said "Hard luck" to them after a bad performance — and then axed them for the following game.

I tell them frequently that they shouldn't worry when I'm giving them stick because that proves that I'm still interested in them. I'm still concerned about them as players and concerned about what they can give the club. The time to worry is when I stop moaning at them. If I stop shouting at a player then he can have a problem. There are only two reasons I would have for not bawling him out — one is that he has been absolutely magnificent and his performance has been beyond criticism. That has never happened in my time as a manager with any player, incidentally. Or he is not good enough. If the second is the case then he is on his way out of the club. The time for players to get uptight is when I stop biting their ears.

Of course, eventually you hit a further problem and that is when a player is not willing to think for himself. In a sense that is our fault as managers and coaches. We have bred a generation of robots — players who won't accept responsibility, who look towards the dugout at all times for instructions because they are afraid to rely on their own judgment. I can be as guilty as the next one of thinking for players. Yet the more thinking a manager does for his players then the less they will do for themselves. They will simply opt out. It would be better to get back to the old days when a manager's responsibility ended once the players crossed the touchline for the start of a game. It was up to the players then, not the managers or the coaches. I believe we would get more entertainment if that happened again. If players reacted instinctively to situations during a game rather than defer to the dugout it would encourage more adventurous play.

When I was a player with Hamilton, just starting out as a teenager, the manager Johnny Low didn't have a great deal to do with the training of the team. Tactics were worked out among the players. That was the way the game was then. Managers, more or less, were a front. Even when I first moved to Clyde and Dawson Walker, who had been Scotland's World Cup trainer, was in charge, I expected to suddenly learn a lot. I didn't. All we did until John Prentice took over as manager was play practice games. Nothing much else happened apart from games and lapping.

What you picked up came from the older players. I used to sit in a corner at Hamilton with Jim Samson and Sam Hastings, scared to open my mouth. The older players there at that time were Wilson Humphries and Johnny Aitkenhead who had been with Motherwell and Rab Quinn who had had a spell with Celtic. You wouldn't say boo to them because they had been around in the game. They were seasoned professionals and we were just raw kids. But what we learned about the game came from them because managers were not as involved then as in many ways they have to be now. Personally I think the game was better back then in many ways. Maybe I'm getting old or something but today we seem to have taken the game away from the only people who really matter. The fans don't enjoy the game as much as they used to do. Basically I don't think that a lot of them realise fully what is going on. Managers and coaches have stolen the game away from them. We have pushed it on to a higher plane tactically and we have forgotten that the fans have to come with us. If they don't then we are failing in our duty to the game.

Maybe it's time to get back to the old days and the old ways, back to when teams were made up only of defenders and forwards. After all, the only things that really matter on the park are the ball and the goalposts — we have drifted away from that kind of thinking and made the game far too complicated. All the new terms which have come into play simply give players an opportunity to hide a little more. Half of them want to be "sweepers" and the other half want to be midfield players. What is a midfield player? Really, I'm asking that seriously! It's a crazy term and it's been going on for far too long.

We have to go back if we want the game to improve. We have to hand the game back to the fans and forget about the different systems and numbers games that we use. I'm one of the worst offenders and I admit that — but I'd like to change things. In the old days when a player was handed a number two jersey then he knew he was going to be playing against number eleven. More important, the people on the terracings knew that too. They understood that and they expected that and they saw that. Now we involve ourselves in all sorts of variations on the

POPULARITY IS OUT

It might be the one that got away — or else it's Jim McLean explaining how close a scoring try was. (Courtesy of D.C. Thomson.)

numbers in a bid to confuse the opposing manager or his players. The confusion only lasts five minutes before they adjust or you adjust to what they have done. I doubt if it's worth it even though I do play the game myself.

It used to be that there were five people on the park who were forwards and who were expected to score goals. The other five were defenders who had to stop the opposition scoring goals. It was as simple as that — Bill Shankly always maintained that football was a simple game and he was right. We are the people who have complicated it. Players think defensively most of the time in the present-day set-up. There have been times when I've asked my players how many of them see their job as totally defensive when the opposition get the ball. Sometimes you get the whole eleven of them saying that they should be defending. The modern game has made them think that way. But you will never get the whole eleven saying they should be attacking or scoring goals when you have possession. I think that is significant.

JOUSTING WITH GIANTS

From the old-fashioned set-up where you had five players who expected to be attacking you are now down to a situation where you may have just two or three players in a team who think that way. Quite often a manager will play with just two men up and two others in the wide channels. In that set up I'd bet only *two* would reckon they were expected to score. There may be some midfield players who will say that they are looking for goals but there are not too many of them about and I certainly can't find any of them.

When we played Gothenburg in the UEFA Cup final I liked the way they numbered their players. OK, it wasn't exactly the same way it used to be in this country. But it went straight through the team in 4-4-2 formation. The back four players, for instance, were 2-3-4-5. You couldn't make it any simpler. It's maybe a small point but I think it's one that the fans would appreciate. They knew where the Gothenburg players were playing. They didn't have to work out for themselves what position the number two was — he was the right-back. That's the way it should be.

If there has been any real change in me over the past few years — and I feel there has been — it goes back to the time I spent as assistant manager to Jock Stein with the Scotland squad. He took me out of my goldfish bowl at Tannadice where I was just push, push, pushing at the players day after day and made me realise that there was a whole world outside my own club. I was also able to realise that my players at Tannadice were possibly better than I had given them credit for. At international level you were working with the top players in the whole country and my players stood up well in comparison to players from other clubs. I saw them in a different light. I went back to the club still looking for more from them but knowing deep down that they were *good* players. I don't necessarily see anything wrong with demanding more even from good players and I still do it. But I believed in them more and I think that I believed in myself more. Jock Stein gave me that little bit extra confidence. It was a tremendous factor, very important for someone like me who is beset by so many self doubts.

After my spell with the World Cup squad I became more relaxed. I had the knowledge then that the training routines we use at Tannadice and the tactical awareness which exists in the club were things to be proud of. I am proud of it. Very proud. But I was ashamed of the way I had handled the job Jock gave me . . .

Chapter Seven

A HANGER-ON WITH SCOTLAND

I spent around four years as assistant manager to Jock Stein with the Scotland international squad — and I was nothing more than a hanger-on in almost all of that time. I'm still ashamed today of the way I did that job, and ashamed that I might have let Jock Stein down after he had shown a great deal of faith in me and in my ability as a coach. Quite honestly, I was a disgrace as an assistant manager.

There was no way I contributed enough to the role Jock handed me. If anything I gained more from taking the job than either Jock or Scotland did. My confidence was boosted for a start. My view on the game was widened because I moved out of the confines of Dundee United and Tannadice. My knowledge of world football was improved because I had a view from the dugout of the top games and the top names in international football. I gained experience of a World Cup which I would never have had if Jock had not taken me with him to Spain for the finals. And, at the end of the day, I gave scarcely anything back to him. I could have done far more to help him. I should have done far more to help him. Instead I cheated him and I cheated the players and I cheated myself.

Looking back, I realise now that I approached the job in the wrong way. Possibly because of my own lack of confidence, I didn't try to assert myself. It was in my mind that I was asked to be assistant manager, number two, and therefore I did not want to ever be accused of undermining Jock. It worried me that if I pushed myself forward at training or at team talks then it might be misunderstood. People might take the view that I was trying to make a name for myself at Jock Stein's expense. That was always nagging away at the back of my mind and so when I had anything to say I said it to Jock in private. We had occasional disagreements but they were between us. Publicly I stayed strictly in the background. Even with the players I stood behind Jock. He was the manager and I believed then that my role had to be completely secondary.

Now I would handle the whole thing in a much different way. I would want to make a contribution if the clock was turned back and I had the chance all over again. I would offer to take more training sessions, make my voice heard in the team talks, contribute something to the job. Instead, I took only about ten training sessions in all the years I had the job. Some of them were good, one or two were brilliant, but at no time did I take enough of the work-outs. Jock took most of them himself but I know now that I should have contributed so much more to the whole set-up.

Sometimes I wonder what my own players thought about it all, because in these years with Scotland I was a Jekyll and Hyde manager. I worked in my own way still at Tannadice, yet with Scotland I sat quietly in the background. Not one of these Scotland players — apart from the Dundee United men in the squad — knew what kind of manager I was at club level. None of them experienced any of the dressing-room scenes which are a regular part of life with any club. It didn't happen because I didn't allow it to happen. I deferred to Jock because I reckoned that was what the assistant manager's job should be — simply to be there to help the manager when he needed help and to exchange views with him when he wanted that.

We disagreed on some things, on the approach to some of the games, or the tactics used in some of them. If I thought he was wrong then I would tell him. Sometimes we did not see eye to eye at all but I know that he appreciated the chance of an argument over some aspect of the team selection or tactics we were going to use. Once I suggested to him that he would be better getting rid of me and appointing someone else who would agree more with him on the various aspects of the squad and the set-up. I still remember him telling me: "I don't want a 'yes' man. It would be very easy for me to go out and get a 'yes' man — but what good would he be to me? That would be no use to me at all. People who

Back from the World Cup finals in Spain in 1982, a sad faced Jim McLean while behind him Dave Narey signs autographs for the waiting fans. (Courtesy of D.C. Thomson.)

JOUSTING WITH GIANTS

Three managerial giants come together to salute Dundee United boss Jim McLean at a testimonial dinner in his honour. Joining Jim are Alex Ferguson, now with Manchester United, the late Scotland manager Jock Stein and Lawrie McMenemy. (Courtesy of D.C. Thomson.)

would agree with me no matter what was going on are ten-a-penny. I want an opinion from you, a personal opinion. At the end of the day I'll listen to you but I'll make up my own mind. I would not have you here if you weren't ready to state your views plainly and honestly. That's what I need."

Really, though, he needed more. He needed me devoting myself heart and soul to the job the way I did at club level. I didn't provide that for him. I took far more out of the job than I ever put into it . . . and I learned a lot from Jock Stein about the game, and about handling the media side of management. He taught me more than anyone else about that side of things. At international level, particularly during a World Cup, that is a most demanding part of an international team manager's job.

There were occasions in Spain when I wondered how Jock managed to handle all the different and demanding aspects of the job. He had games to face, tactics to work out, teams to pick. Yet he also had to speak to journalists and television people three or four times every day. It was an exhausting schedule for anyone and I had nothing but

A HANGER-ON WITH SCOTLAND

admiration for the way he was able to do all of these things. I like to think that I've mellowed in my own relations with the Press and if I have then it's partly due to picking up on press relations from Jock Stein. He opened my eyes to a side of management which I'd never been very good at.

I learned other things too. I remember one of our disagreements which came before a Wembley game against England. Jock picked the team and decided that we would play with Davie Provan of Celtic and Notts Forest's John Robertson as our wingers or wide men. There was no way that I could see that working. Not on the mud heap that the Wembley pitch was going to be for this match. Neither Davie Provan nor John Robertson were defensively minded players. They were not the types who would come back up the park to fill in for the team. Even on the way to the game from our hotel in Harpenden I was arguing with

Jim McLean enjoys a joke with the late Jock Stein and Scotland masseur Jimmy Steele as they prepare to board a flight at Glasgow Airport during the United manager's stint as Scotland number two. (Courtesy of D.C. Thomson.)

Jock about the team selection — but he knew better than I did. We won. A John Robertson penalty eventually gave us that victory but the team played the way Jock had planned and played well. That afternoon was another part of my learning process, another time when I was able to watch how Jock Stein worked with his teams and his individual players.

Eventually I left the job. There were various reasons, including my personal troubles with the Scottish Football Association which saw me banned from sitting in the dugout. It was going to make for embarrassment to everyone if I continued in the Scotland job, working for the SFA in a role which they had banned me from performing with my own club. My old mate Alex Ferguson was appointed as Jock's assistant in my place — and Fergie did a far better job as assistant manager to Scotland than I had done.

Before accepting the appointment he phoned me to find out exactly what the job entailed. It was the kind of thoroughness you expect of Fergie and I think he recognised from what I told him the mistakes I had made in the job. He went about it in a different way and because of that he was a better number two than I had been. He did more to help Jock than I had and finally, of course, he took over as manager for Mexico after Jock's tragic death in Wales.

I didn't envy Fergie that job. The Scotland job is not one I have been offered, and it's definitely not one I would want to take on. Rumours linked me with the job after the World Cup in Mexico — but under no circumstances would I have taken the job at that time. I was not in the least interested in the position when it was vacant after the World Cup games in Mexico and I honestly believe that Andy Roxburgh has taken the job at a really bad time. It is never an easy task but Andy has it tougher than anyone else has ever had it. There is no doubt in my mind about that. Coming back after a World Cup which brought another disappointment is always bad enough. Coming back to the increased number of games in the Premier League made it impossible. There was never the slightest chance of qualifying for the finals of the European Championship in West Germany.

The demands on our top players are always enormous — but they have been increased. Forty-four League games is crazy. How can you look for the top players — and these are the players you depend on in the international team — coping with all of that? Especially as being in Mexico created special problems for them all. Playing at altitude and in the heat drained the players. Most of them returned from that particular trip without any appetite for the longer than usual grind of

McLean is seen here in his role as Scotland coach along with skipper Archie Gemmill — but the Tannadice manager feels he did not do enough in that job. (Courtesy of D.C. Thomson.)

Premier League matches. Yet Andy Roxburgh had to go to these same players and pick them up and start all over again with fiercely competitive international matches.

JOUSTING WITH GIANTS

Anyone with any sense would not have wanted the job at that particular time. Billy McNeill was rumoured to be interested but I would have doubted if that was the case once he examined the situation closely. The odds were stacked high against whoever took on the job as international team boss. Probably I'll be criticised for saying this. Some people will reckon that my attitude is tantamount to chickening out of a responsibility toward my country. I don't see it that way. To me you have to examine every situation surrounding a job and any manager taking on the Scotland job after Mexico was landing himself in trouble. No one wants to put themselves in a worse situation than they are in.

I admire Andy Roxburgh for taking it on but I'm not sure he would have accepted the job offer if he had realised all the problems and all the pitfalls which make the job such an impossible one. I looked at them and my mind was made up. If the SFA had asked me to take over I would have turned them down.

I feel sympathy for Andy Roxburgh in the criticism he has had since taking on the job but it is something that all managers come to expect. None of us like it but often there is very little we can do about it. It is unfair most of the time and in the case of Andy Roxburgh it is extremely unfair when you examine the situation he took over. There were the extra games, the hangover from Mexico, and the fact that Kenny Dalglish and Graeme Souness were drifting out of the international scene at the same time. Any manager knows that if players are not there then there is very little you can do. For example, I don't accept that Jim McLean is responsible for everything that has happened at Dundee United down through the years that I have been manager. No one can say that. Any improvement in a club or in an international team comes because of the quality of player out on the field. Neither Jock Stein nor Alex Ferguson nor Jim McLean could make quality players out of ordinary players. Perhaps good managers work that little bit harder than other managers. Perhaps they can get players to express their capabilities that bit better and encourage the ordinary players to play within their limitations. But you cannot make these players into the exceptional players that top teams require if they are going to be successful. That's not on.

The biggest problem that Andy Roxburgh faces is that true international-class players are not available at this time. We don't have the kind of player who can hold his own at World Cup level in great enough numbers. There is not a great deal that Andy Roxburgh can do about that. Not a great deal that any manager would be able to do about it!

Losing Dalglish and Souness, two very influential players, was another blow. They were both players who would have gone into any team in the world. Graeme Souness is one of the best players I have ever seen in my life. Down through all the years I have been involved in the game as a player and as a manager I cannot think of anyone to match him. Kenny was in exactly the same category — and yet their contributions to the international team were not as high as I expected them to be. They were both world-class players and yet I did not see them playing at world-class standards for Scotland. There is no way that I'm criticising either of them for that. It's part and parcel of the course. There are other players who have been the same. They perform magnificently at club level, even on a European stage at times, but they can't reach the same level when they join the international squad.

I saw this at close range when I worked with Jock. Playing in the international set-up is more difficult than playing at club level. We are so far behind in our preparations compared to the Continental teams. There appears to be a lack of planning, a lack of forethought when it comes down to giving the international team as good a chance as the opposition of qualifying for the various competitions. I can remember Jock Stein pointing out to me how it often happened that the Premier League's hardest fixtures seemed to fall on the weekend before an important match. That's when you would have Celtic playing Rangers or Aberdeen playing Dundee United — and yet these were the teams we were relying on for players. We lean on the top clubs and then find that they have vital games a few days before an equally vital international match. Jock always maintained that this would never happen to a top European international side. Indeed, you tend to find that the entire League programme is scrapped in countries like Italy and Spain and West Germany. While in Russia, Dynamo Kiev, who provide the bulk of the players for the national team, find themselves favoured when the domestic league programme is on. It would seem natural but it doesn't seem that way to the Scottish League. Sometimes I think we have qualified for the World Cup finals in spite of the attitude of officials here in Scotland.

Sometimes, too, the expectations of the fans are too high. I don't think many countries can boast a better, more loyal, support than Scotland has had down the years. But there are occasions when that can bring problems. People *expect* Scotland to qualify for the World Cup every four years now. Yet there was a whole period of time from

1958 until 1974 that we were never able to reach the finals. Since then there has been a fantastic run by the team. We may have done badly in the European Championships but we have done magnificently in the World Cup qualifying rounds. Starting when we qualified for the finals in West Germany in 1974, we have been able to get to Argentina in 1978, Spain in 1982 when I was with the squad as assistant manager, and then Mexico in 1986. Soon it will be time to start the qualifying games once again — and Andy Roxburgh will find that the Scots fans put a high priority on the World Cup. They will want to see the team in Italy in 1990 and as I said earlier they will simply *expect* that the side qualifies.

I wish Andy all the luck in the world for these games when they arrive. He will need that. He will also need a more enlightened approach to the matches from the Scottish League when they are planning their fixtures to cover the qualifying period.

Honestly, I think it's been a miracle that a small country like Scotland has been able to reach the finals on four successive occasions. People outside the game have no idea of just how difficult the international scene is. When you are a club manager you have the chance to work out with your players every day. When you are with the international squad you see them for two or three days every few months. We will never see the day when we are allowed lengthy get-togethers, the luxury that so many of the foreign coaches get with the national teams. The demands of our domestic programme and the power of club football make that impossible. But if we are to be even reasonably successful as a nation some kind of compromise must be reached. It is far too much to expect a team manager to blend players into a really solid unit when he has only a short time available to him for training. Even when the players are together you find that the physical demands at club level have been so rigorous that training sessions cannot always be as concentrated as you would like.

Basically, with all the problems that exist, it is a job I would never want to tackle. I used to see the frustration that Jock Stein felt after a poor result when he realised that the following day the players would be back with their clubs and he would not have the chance to hold any kind of post-mortem. Probably that is one of the worst things of all. With a club you can go over mistakes when they are still fresh in the players' minds — with the Scotland squad you may have to wait for two months or even more to point out the errors which might have cost a match. By then time has blunted the memories of both players and managers. It just doesn't work.

Jim McLean and the late Scotland boss Jock Stein go over a training routine in Portugal prior to the World Cup finals in Spain.

All I say is that the critics should remember some of these problems before attacking Andy Roxburgh. He has the hardest job of any of us, particularly at the time he was invited to take over. These extra eight Premier League games were killers for our top players and they are the men Scotland has to depend on.

Chapter Eight

AN AFTERNOON OF FEAR IN ROME

Sometimes recent achievements tend to take people's thoughts away from past performances and that's only natural. But, while reaching the final of the UEFA Cup was an outstanding display by a club as small as Dundee United is, that campaign followed seasons of European experience, seasons of hardening into a team able to handle the special pressures that the Continent throws up.

It wasn't only in the Nou Camp in Barcelona or the Boekelberg Stadium in Moenchengladbach that Dundee United came of age in Europe. There had been other matches, other stadiums, other seasons when the team had been able to grow in stature and, hopefully, add something to the reputation of Scottish soccer. There were games in Belgium and in Holland. In West Germany and in France. In Austria and in Sweden. In Czechoslovakia and in Yugoslavia. In Poland and in Rumania. We grew up on so many foreign fields and gradually we put together the playing pattern which helped bring us some successes in the European tournaments.

In the main our games were in the UEFA Cup, which had started life as the Fairs Cities Cup and was called that when United made their European debut away back in 1966 — beating, incidentally, Barcelona! As I write this we have played around 70 games in the competition, more than any other Scottish club. And some of the results we gained

AN AFTERNOON OF FEAR IN ROME

A night off as Jim McLean relaxes with Dundee United director George Grant, the late chairman Johnstone Grant and his backroom men Walter Smith and Gordon Wallace. Smith's departure for Rangers was a "body blow" to the club, recalls McLean. (Courtesy of D.C. Thomson.)

in these games provided us with the pedigree to take on the great names of Europe when we were battling our way to the two-legged final against Gothenburg. I can remember a stunning shot from Frank Kopel putting out Anderlecht of Belgium . . . and the night we went to Monte Carlo and broke the bank. We shocked the French side that day by hammering in five goals against them away from home. There was a Paul Hegarty goal against Werder Bremen in West Germany which pushed us into the quarter-finals of the competition that season. It's a whole rich tapestry of memories, some warm and friendly because of victories gained or performances to be proud of, some bitter and sad because of decisions which went against us, or travel problems which turned trips into nightmares as we had to make our way to the very frontiers of European football.

But there is only one when I felt myself in real physical danger. Only one when I felt myself under constant threat. That was in Rome on an April afternoon in 1984 when the Olympic Stadium throbbed with hate and I was the target for the abuse of the Italian fans and the Roma players. It was an experience I would not have wished on my worst enemy and an experience, quite honestly, I didn't believe could have happened in this day and age. But it did. And I genuinely feared for my safety. It was a dreadful end to a season which had started in the confident after-glow of winning our first Premier League title. Naturally, as champions of Scotland we were to play in the European Cup, the Champions' Cup as it is formally called, and the tournament which is the most prestigious club competition in Europe. In fact, it may be the best in the world. The year before, we had reached the last eight of the UEFA Cup before losing to the one goal of the two ties to Bohemians Prague. That experience had set us up for a crack at the number one trophy and when we were drawn against Hamrun Spartans of Malta in the first round we all felt that, perhaps, things were going to go right for us. It was the type of draw that any team welcomes in the first round, a comfortable means of playing your way in early in the season. The first leg was away from home which also suited us. We soon realised, though, that the only problem for us in getting this game out of the way was to be the playing pitch. The notorious surface of the National Stadium in Malta had upset many teams in the past and while UEFA had given it clearance as suitable for matches falling under their jurisdiction we were under no illusions. Looking back now that surface even made the Ullevi Stadium look good. It was baked hard by the Mediterranean sun and was scorched by deep ruts made by the tractors which had been used apparently to bring the surface up to the standards demanded by the European bosses.

To add to the worries we might have over that we also faced the thought of going on to the pitch second that afternoon. Before us there was an earlier clash in a European double-header — Rangers travelled out to the island with us and were playing a European Cup Winners Cup game against Valetta. The pitch, bad enough to begin with, wasn't going to be helped any by another game taking place immediately before our European Cup debut. Still, there was little we could do about it. The Maltese wanted the two games played together and had the blessing of the European Union for their plan. We went along with it and sat in the sunshine for part of the first match which saw Rangers destroy Valetta 8-0 in a game which saw Dave McPherson, now of Hearts but then a teenage Rangers' defender, score four goals.

We did not expect a goal feast in our own game because, despite what Rangers had managed, I don't believe there are too many games now where you get these high scores. As it turned out I was right as regards our own match. Hamrun had had a warning from the Rangers game. They had seen their island rivals demolished by a Scottish side. They had no intention of being victims in the same way. They played

AN AFTERNOON OF FEAR IN ROME

tidily and they defended and they made sure that we were not going to be allowed to run amok.

All that counted in the end was a victory and a decent performance and we were able to provide that. When John Reilly scored the first goal within a few minutes then people did expect another rout but it was not to be and we didn't let that affect our approach to the game. Eamonn Bannon and Derek Stark added other goals and when we flew home the following day we knew that we were safely in the second round of the tournament even though there was a match still to come at Tannadice.

The next game, at home, brought us a comfortable follow-up to the first leg — another three-goal win giving us a 6-0 aggregate score with the goals this time around coming from Ralph Milne, who scored twice, and Billy Kirkwood. But the worry which hit us that night came from an injury to Paul Sturrock which was to keep him out of the next round tie against the formidable Belgian champions, Standard Liege.

We had played them before, five years earlier, and had lost then to the solitary goal scored in the two-legged tie. Belgian football was admired throughout most of Europe and their own players and imported stars from other European countries made sure that their clubs were difficult opponents for anyone. Indeed that same season Standard's great rivals from Brussels, Anderlecht, were to reach the final of the UEFA Cup where they would lose out to Spurs on penalties.

We had no doubts that Standard would provide us with problems and we had players still in the team who could remember the earlier clashes — and the worries we had then! In fact, seven of the players who were to play in the European Cup ties had been in action against the Belgians on the previous occasion — plus my assistant manager Walter Smith had also played in the Fairs Cup matches. The players, though, who had been in action before were Hamish McAlpine, Billy Kirkwood, John Holt, Paul Hegarty, Dave Narey, Ralph Milne and Davie Dodds. If Paul Sturrock had not been injured then it would have given us yet another player with experience of facing up to the Belgians.

They had changed a great deal more — just three men had survived from the Fairs Cup year, the goalkeeper Preud'homme, and two others, Plessers and Poel. In the first round they had scored eight goals against Athlone at home and had taken that tie on an 11-4 aggregate. They now had Simon Tahamata, the former Ajax player, in their line-up as well as the giant West German international striker, Horts

Hrubesch. It was the kind of game you might have hoped to avoid so early in the tournament but you always realise deep down that if you can get one good draw then you cannot look for a great deal more in any of the European competitions. We had had our piece of luck with the visit to Malta — I didn't look for anything more. That way we were saved the inevitable disappointments. In any case, once you have found your feet, tested the water so to speak, then you know that there is little alternative but to get on with things. We had our own problems — and Britain's other representatives, Liverpool, had their problems too by being drawn to face Atletico Bilbao, the champions of Spain. The Champions Cup is that type of tournament. But while it produces the supreme tests for any clubs wanting to build a reputation for themselves at the highest level, then it also provides a stage where players can show what they can do, where teams can parade their knowledge and skills and their tactical know-how.

Over the two ties against Standard Liege my players picked up the challenge better than they have ever done before or since. Over the two games, a fortnight apart as always, they produced the most perfect performance out of all the 70 or so ties we have ever played in Europe. Most of you will have realised by now, if you had not had a fair idea before, that I am not the kind of manager who is given to singing the praises of his players too much. This time there was no other way I could describe the performances they produced over the 180 minutes of football. It was as if all the lessons they had learned in previous years, and all the teaching they had had from myself and the coaching staff, had reached fruition. As team displays go I cannot think of any to match them in all the years I've been with the club. For once I could afford to sit back and to enjoy some of the play, relax and savour the achievements of the club, because out there in front of us was the realisation of hours and days and years of training and talking, of listening and learning, of practising and preparing, of working and waiting.

The waiting was made worth while in Belgium and then again at Tannadice in the return. Over the two games we defeated the Belgian side tactically. We defeated them individually. We defeated them by playing the Continental game better than they were able to do themselves. Over there we controlled the tie. It went the way we wanted it to go. It took the pattern we imposed on the match. Rarely, if at all, did we look in any danger of defeat.

Then came the return and the worry leading up to that game that

AN AFTERNOON OF FEAR IN ROME

That Tannadice partnership which was broken up when Walter Smith left to take over as number two to Graeme Souness at Ibrox. Here Smith shouts advice from the dugout as Jim McLean puzzles over the next move. (Courtesy of D.C. Thomson.)

perhaps our form could not be sustained for the second leg. That was soon washed away as we again established control and in another superb performance we were able to win 4-0 in front of a crowd of 18,500. Ralph Milne scored another two goals that night, Paul Hegarty grabbed another and Davie Dodds joined in — all men who had played before against Standard. They all enjoyed the feeling of revenge for being knocked out by the Belgians in the UEFA Cup in the very first round in 1978!

So at the first time of asking we had reached the last eight of the European Cup — and our interest stretched several months into the future because of the winter break which sees just two games played in the two top Cups before Christmas. Indeed the games are usually over by early November, with the quarter-finals not taking place until March. We had all that time from November until after the turn of the year to look at the other teams in the tourney before the draw was made. The line-up was just as formidable as you would have expected — Liverpool and ourselves were there and then you had Dynamo Minsk from Russia; Dinamo Bucharest from Rumania; Dynamo Berlin from East Germany; Roma from Italy; Rapid Vienna from Austria and Benfica from Portugal.

Although the winter shut-down tends to affect teams who have long breaks from their season because of adverse weather conditions we still did not relish a trip behind the Iron Curtain with all of the travel problems that entailed. If at all possible then, we wanted to avoid any of the trio of teams from Eastern Europe. That left us with a choice of four others — three of them among Europe's aristocrats — Liverpool, Roma and Benfica. Then there was Rapid Vienna, solid enough opposition but without the feared reputation of these others. Yet they had beaten the French champions Nantes in the first round and they had then disposed of Bohemians Prague from Czechoslovakia the next time out. If they did not have an outstanding reputation as a team they did have a scattering of Austrian international players, including striker Hans Krankl and the Czech star Anton Panenka, a free kick specialist who would, on his day, threaten the best defences in the world. The going was getting tougher but, still, when we drew Rapid we were not too unhappy. Travel problems would be slight. Hotel and food would suit the players and we were going to have a chance of reaching the semi-finals. Who could ask for more?

Anyhow, by now we were establishing something of a reputation ourselves. In our four games we had yet to lose a goal and we had managed to score ten. Rapid would have noticed that about us just as we had noticed that the veteran Panenka had been able to score three of their goals against Nantes in the opening round, and that the other veteran, the striker Krankl, had scored the goal at home which took them through against the Czechs.

We prepared carefully, as always, going to watch them playing in their domestic league. Again we had been happy that the first game was to be played in Vienna. That was always something which pleased me

AN AFTERNOON OF FEAR IN ROME

— I still prefer it even though things worked out well for us in the ties against Barcelona and Borussia recently when that didn't happen. It's just that I feel more comfortable coming to our own pitch knowing exactly what has to be done to get us through.

It was a nice hat-trick as far as I was concerned that it should happen in all the European Cup rounds, but no matter how kind a draw may be, or how much you reckon the omens favour you, the games have still to be won. We knew that this would be hard and that's exactly how it turned out even though we exploded into a dream start when our fullback Derek Stark crashed in a 30-yard shot which beat their goalkeeper Feurer to give us an early lead. It was the away goal we had wanted — and the away goal which Rapid had no doubt been determined to stop us getting. Yet, in a strange way it almost worked against us a little in that match. For Rapid knew from the beginning that they had to go all out in attack and we were left trying to weather these non-stop raids and also hanging on to the valuable goal lead we had taken. It was late in the second half before we allowed them the goal chances they needed to win the game. Hagmayr and Krancjar were the scorers but as we flew home we were the team in the driving seat. That away goal meant a single goal at Tannadice would take us into the semi-finals. If we won by 1-0 then the Austrians would go out on the away goals counting double in the event of a draw rule. As long as we could stop them scoring and so cancelling out our advantage we were heading for a place in the last four. Up to that time we had still to concede a goal at home — the two goals in Vienna were the only ones we had lost in the Cup — and so we went into the second leg at Tannadice with that knowledge to back us up.

Seventeen and a half thousand people were in Tannadice to see Davie Dodds get that goal and then watch us live through the nervous near 70 minutes remaining before the final whistle blew and we knew that we had achieved a great breakthrough for the club. On the same night, less than 70 miles further north, Aberdeen under the management of my pal Alex Ferguson were making their own way through to the semi-final of the European Cup Winners Cup with a victory over Ujpest Dozsa of Hungary. That meant Scotland having two teams in the semi-finals of major tournaments in Europe, though not for the first time. It had happened before when Rangers and Celtic had semi-final celebrations together.

But it was an important landmark for what had been dubbed the "New Firm" of Dundee United and Aberdeen. Here we were, two provincial clubs who had taken on the top teams from Glasgow at home — and now were taking on the top teams in Europe — and we were winning on both fronts! Fergie used to always say to me that we needed each other in the fight for domestic honours. Against Aberdeen we would fight as hard as we did against anyone and they were the same when they were facing us. We were bitter rivals as we chased the honours in Scotland. Yet, I knew what Fergie had meant. We had to be able to take points off the Old Firm, or knock them out of the Cup competitions. If we were both doing it then we were helping each other and loosening the stranglehold that the teams from Parkhead and Ibrox had had on the Scottish game for so long. Now, apart from the successes at home, we were marching into Europe shoulder to shoulder so to speak. It was an important night for both clubs and an auspicious night for Scotland. For two provincial clubs with limited support to scale these heights together was unbelievable.

Yet there was so much agony to follow that night's ecstasy as far as we were concerned. So much trouble, so much scandal. So many broken dreams. And a feeling of fear and distaste which will stay with me for as long as I live.

In my home in Broughty Ferry there is a video of the second match in Rome when we played the Italian champions. It sits there gathering dust because it has never been watched. Something deep down inside me stops me from looking at the scenes in the Olympic Stadium that April afternoon. Normally I would have watched and analysed how we had played. Normally I would have looked at that video a dozen times or more. I have not watched a single minute of it — and I don't know if I ever will. It is there as a reminder of the sick side of soccer, a side I never want to see again. That day brought me more misery and more heartache than even the loss of the UEFA Cup final. Because the sorrow I felt was not only for me. Nor only for my players. It was for the game of football itself as I sat through the hate and venom, which spilled from the terracings of that giant stadium long before the kick-off until we finally left under police escort for the airport and our flight home.

It didn't begin in Rome, of course. It began almost immediately the final whistle sounded at the end of the first-leg game at Tannadice. That is when the propaganda started, when the campaign of hate against the team and against myself built up until it reached its crescendo in the Olympic Stadium two weeks later. Perhaps I handled it badly. Perhaps now I would react differently to the allegations which

United manager McLean and his right hand man Gordon Wallace walk out on to the field at Tannadice after the Scots had lost their second leg game against Gothenburg in the final of the UEFA Cup. (Courtesy of D.C. Thomson.)

were hurled at me by the Italian Press within minutes of the game ending. It was then that they accused our players of taking drugs, of using stimulants. Of course I lost the place. I couldn't quite believe this was happening to me and to the club. We had never known or experienced anything like this before. So I blew up when perhaps, now, I would be a little more politic in answering the questions. The next day I was able to joke about it, telling the Press that I just wished the players were on the same every week. In every game. We laughed it off together then — but the Italians hadn't laughed. They had written stories that the Dundee United players had taken drugs in order to be able to beat the Italian champions.

If I had been more alert to the questions then maybe the whole thing would not have blown up in the same way as it did. Yet, even now, saying that I wonder. Because at the end of the day it looked like a calculated campaign whipped up against myself and the players before we could get to Rome and that second leg. It still baffles me why people who are so gifted and so talented should stoop so low just to get the results they want. Don't get me wrong, I'm not blaming the coach Nils Liedholm for any of this — he was a gentleman. But others in the club seemed ready to give support to the scandalously dishonest claims made against us. It hurt me then and it hurts me now to look back at that time. To some extent we were confused by all that happened even though the drugs claims warned us to some extent of what we were going to be up against.

Maybe they could not handle the defeat they had to suffer at Tannadice. After all, they had a team of stars, a multi-talented team carefully put together at enormous cost to win the Italian Championship and restore some of Roma's faded grandeur. Then, with the European final being set for the city, there was extra pressure from the club directors and from the fans for the team to be in that final. On their own ground. In their own city. They felt they were destined to win the trophy.

Of course, we had other ideas and that night at Tannadice we dominated the game. We didn't let the reputations of some of their big name players worry us. They had Conti and Graziani from Italy's World Cup-winning team in Spain two years earlier. They had the outstanding Brazilian midfielders Falcao and Cerezo who had been so magnificent in that same tournament when I had seen them at first hand against Scotland in the qualifying game in Seville which we lost 4-1 after Dave Narey had scored a brilliant opener for us. They had

AN AFTERNOON OF FEAR IN ROME

other talented players who had been capped for their country and we recognised the talents of Righetti and Di Bartolemei, their play-maker, and Pruzzo, who was the striking partner for Graziani. In Dundee Falcao was unfit and could not play — but in the hectic cup-tie atmosphere we set out to create that night it is doubtful if he would have relished the action too much. His kind of flowing, polished, patient football was not made for the all-action Scottish game we used to upset them.

It worked for us. We won 2-0 with goals from Derek Stark and Davie Dodds and there we were with our record of not losing a game or a goal at home intact. While we won well we almost made the score even higher. There were chances which came to us and were missed or else the Italian goalkeeper Tancredi was able to save or a late intervention by a defender just foiled our forwards. It was another notable victory for the team and one which we thought we could relish for at least a few days.

Then the poison began to drip and the drugs claims which were totally nonsensical set us up for the kind of hostility we had never had to face before. Certainly in other places we had been under pressure from opposition fans. It's fairly normal to have lighted cigarettes thrown into your dugout or even thrown at the goalkeeper. And once, in Nis in Yugoslavia when we were playing Radnicki in the UEFA Cup quarter-final, we had even suffered iron bolts being thrown at the players and at ourselves. The missiles thrown at us in Rome didn't reach that dangerous level but the build-up was so much more sinister. So much more deliberate. We felt as if we were being fed to the lions — and every little thing I did or said was being blown up and distorted.

The trouble was that I fell partly into the trap because I was naïve. I had not expected this. It scarred me, you know. Until now I have never talked about it because the memories are so bad.

As I've said, we had experienced intimidation before, or attempted intimidation, but never at this level. Roma and their fans and the Italian media wanted them in the final which was to be played the following month. I'm sure that the UEFA bosses wanted Roma to be there too. It was such a natural moneyspinner, such a tremendous spectacle. Would they have wanted unfashionable Dundee United instead?

But that's what we wanted, and unfortunately we were the men who stood between Roma and that season's dream final. That had a great deal to do with what went on. There are times I feel that if we had been the team to meet Roma in the final then I might not be alive today.

When I say that I'm only exaggerating a little because I did genuinely fear for my safety. When I walked out into that stadium there were banners all around bearing insults directed at me. They booed and jeered me and they threw oranges and drinks at me. The whole atmosphere was frightening — and we could not handle that. It was too much for us because it was the ugly face of football we saw that day and we had never seen it as bad as that before. I never want to even glimpse it again.

The game itself is a blur to me and I've never felt, as I said earlier, the desire to watch it on film. It's best pushed to the back of my mind, partly forgotten at least. Even recalling it now makes me feel strange. The whole episode was distasteful.

The youngest player on the field, Maurice Malpas, was booked in the opening minutes, then Ralph Milne missed a chance and soon the Italians were in command. Pruzzo scored twice for them and the so talented Di Bartolemei sent a penalty kick past Hamish McAlpine and we were out. But the torment didn't end with the whistle. When it blew some of the Italian players rushed towards me as I got up from the bench which had been out in the open on the touchline. I simply kept walking as they screamed abuse at me and then going up the tunnel and back to what I hoped would be the safety of the dressing-rooms I was pelted by missiles from the fans. I suddenly realised that the massive police presence which had been there for our protection earlier had now disappeared. No one was there to make sure that we reached the dressing-room.

All I could do was keep on walking. I knew I could not afford to become involved in a brawl with, for instance, Tancredi who had been the worst of the players who had charged at me. Behind me I could hear scuffles as people tried to attack me. I know now that Walter Smith and our reserve goalkeeper John Gardiner kept them away from me. They saved me from what might have been serious injury — and certainly what would have been the kind of brawl they wanted to drag me into. No one will convince me otherwise that if I had stepped just a little out of line then I would have been the man in trouble. I'm sure that some of the police who had vanished would have made a reappearance and I would have been their target too. I have never known anything like that in my career and I hope I never have to go through it again.

There is no doubt that the players were affected. Almost every one of them dropped below form that day. The atmosphere in the Olympic Stadium caused that — nothing else. We had Malpas booked early on

Jim McLean accepts congratulations from a woman supporter after his team's European Cup win over Roma at Tannadice. (Courtesy of D.C. Thomson.)

and that did make us apprehensive but the referee also chalked off a Roma scoring try which, in other cases, might have stood. So it wasn't a question of the referee beating us. Our own display was what was wrong, with the baiting from the crowd and the hate and hostility which had been whipped up making it a nightmare for all of us.

Later, some time in the next season, there were allegations that the referee that day had been bribed. But you know something? — that didn't interest me when it was first mentioned and it doesn't interest me now. I would be cheating to talk about that because it would be looking for excuses. Maybe something did go on. I don't know and I don't care. All I do know for sure is that we did not play well there. We played well at Tannadice. Possibly we deserved even more than we got from that first game — but we got what we deserved in the Olympic Stadium. Probably ten out of our eleven players didn't reach their normal standards. That is what cost us our place in the European Cup final. People can talk about bribes as long as they like — I still won't pay any attention because it wasn't a factor as far as I was concerned.

Liverpool may have handled it better when they went to the final. They drew 1-1 but then won on penalties. I was glad they did.

Chapter 9

MY LOVE AFFAIR WITH DUNDEE UNITED

Every morning in life I arrive at Tannadice and start switching off lights in the place immediately. It's become something of a joke with the staff at the ground now — maybe even something of a legend to people who have read about me doing this. But I don't care. It happens every day and it will go on happening just as long as I am manager of Dundee United. This club has survived and prospered because it was built on solid foundations. Good housekeeping is the secret at Tannadice. Good housekeeping meant that we balanced the books. Good housekeeping meant that we did not pay lavish salaries to players when the club could not afford to do that. Good housekeeping meant that when it was necessary we sold players — and then used that cash to buy in other players and help with ground improvements. Good housekeeping meant never becoming involved in too many grandiose schemes but keeping our feet on the ground.

The way the club has approached all of these aspects has kept Dundee United healthy financially and successful on the field. I learned early in my career as a manager here that anyone taking on the job had two responsibilities. They had to get a good team on the park — and they had to get their sums right. In a small club with a limited financial base the second is more important than the first, because if you cannot balance the books then you won't be able to put out a top team every week.

JOUSTING WITH GIANTS

So in my first week I began to try to save money for the club and I have never changed. We may have a million pounds in the bank but I'm still putting the lights off and I'm still buying all my own meals. I have never charged this club a single penny for meals or anything else. I pay for my own. Even suits and blazers and flannels I've paid for. Nowadays some of the staff get their lunch at the ground — but I pay for mine. I know that some people will look at this and think that I'm tight-fisted about things — it's not that. They can think what they like. All I know is that a major portion of the job I took on at Tannadice was balancing the books, keeping this club afloat financially, and the directors and myself have been able to do that.

Frankly the directors here have been unbelievable. I have been lucky in the two chairmen I have worked under. First of all there was Johnstone Grant and then George Fox and both were tremendous for me and for this club. By the very fact that they have been number one at the club they have been personally out of pocket — that's the way things are at Tannadice. No one is at this club to make a fortune. All they have looked for is some success — which we have had — and keeping the club among the top teams in Scotland. We have been able to do that too.

But, above all, they have not wanted to see this club plunge into the red. The directors have all been very solid businessmen and I think that it went against the grain for them to go into debt when it might not be necessary. And it certainly would not have been prudent. I suppose they saw other clubs hitting the heights and then failing to sustain success, going lower and lower in the game. It has happened in Scotland and in England. Probably in many other countries too when clubs have glimpsed success and then overextended themselves and finished up in serious trouble. It's amazing just how little time it can take for a club to go from the top to the bottom, from financial well-being to heavy, unmanageable debt.

That could never happen at Tannadice. The ground rules have been laid down and for a long, long time they have followed a sensible course of action. There have been times we have not wanted to sell players but we have had to. There have been other times when I have recommended to the board of directors that they accept a big offer for one of the players and, once they have looked at the financial standing of the team, they have told me that there is no need to sell. I have been overruled in that way by them and I'm sure it will happen again if they think that is what should happen. I don't have the power that a lot of

The beginning of a long serving partnership with Dundee United as manager Jim McLean signs Paul Hegarty who was to go on to captain the team to their League and League Cup successes. (Courtesy of D.C. Thomson.)

people think that I have. I am the manager and I am a member of the board — but I have only the one vote at board meetings like everyone else. There is no question of my getting my own way all the time. Nor would I expect that.

I reckon that every manager needs a good chairman and a dependable board of directors to fall back on. Having the chairmen I have had supporting me has made me a better manager. I'm sure of that. No one needs to have board-room problems when there is a team to run and players to look after. I've been lucky that I have never experienced that kind of trouble. It's just as well — because I would probably have walked out!

From the very outset I made up my mind how the job should be handled in the best possible way for the club and the best possible way for me and the players. I wanted a Dundee-based team to kick off. I didn't want to have players who were travelling back and forward from their homes to training every day from Glasgow or Edinburgh, spending hours either driving or on the train undoing all the good work that came from the training workouts.

When I was interviewed for the job as team manager I made that point to the directors quite forcibly. Looking back to that day, I think that being so insistent on this aspect may have convinced them that I was the man they wanted. One of the first things I said at the interview was that players would not be allowed to travel long distances to play for the club. Either the players had to stay in Dundee where they would be available for training at any time I wanted them — or they would have to leave the club. I couldn't see any way round that and I didn't want to. If I'm honest I have to say that I wanted this desperately because I knew that there were players at Tannadice I would have to work with for long, hard hours in training to get them into my ways. I needed to have them in Dundee, close enough to the ground that they would come in to work whenever I felt they should be coming in. I did not want them disappearing after a couple of hours work in the morning to catch the train back to Glasgow or wherever, sitting around eating Mars bars or sandwiches and drinking coffee, then having to get up early in the morning to catch the train back up to Dundee again. It was not good for them and it was not going to be any good for me either. I wanted them to be able to train hard and work hard and then go home to relax. You get the best results from players who do that. Relaxation after the training can be very important.

The first player I had to get rid of was Alan Gordon who had played for Hearts and who had worked out a special deal for himself when he had joined United a year or so earlier. He had only to train two days a week at Tannadice. The rest of the time he was training in Edinburgh. Now Alan was a good enough player — but he was lazy and that kind of set-up was an obvious problem for me. He had to go and he was sold to Eddie Turnbull at Hibs while I used the money I got from the transfer to buy George Fleming and Pat Gardiner. Besides Alan there were another six or seven players who were travelling back and forward from their homes for training and putting in a lot of miles every week doing it.

Besides the handicap on the footballing side, all this travel was costing the club a pile of money every week. It was ridiculous that they were forking out rail fares to all of these players to journey back and forward four or five times a week. It was a considerable burden on the club and I knew that I had to get rid of it. If I could I would have that travelling cash available for players. It could go to the present staff in increased wages or bonus or eventually be used to help buy players when we needed them.

I lost players because I pursued that "live in Dundee before you play for this club" policy. Yet I still saw it as a very important principle. Some players refused to sign for us when they heard that condition being imposed. Others walked out on the club. One notable loss was Jacky Copland, who finally signed for Alex Ferguson at St Mirren. Then we also had problems with Tom McAdam and John Bourke because they were all in their middle to late twenties and the policy was not going to suit them. It was OK for the younger players — but not for the older group. It was a hurdle we simply had to get over before we started to lay down our plans for the club's long-term future! There were casualties and there were players I could have wept at losing — but I knew that it was the right road for the club. And the directors backed me totally. It was an early sign from them of the co-operation and support that I have been able to enjoy in the years I've spent in the job.

Eventually, of course, with the youth policy we set up the team was almost three-quarters made up of local players. They were recruited in and around Dundee and they stayed there. Others who came from outside the town stayed in a club hostel to begin with and then, afterwards, they moved into their own homes or into "digs". Despite the teething problems and the bitterness which the more established players felt about the change, the policy worked. It not only worked, it paid off. Because these local players became the core of the team which found success in the eighties. It took time — but it was all so worth while. If anything the players who decided to move on because they could not move house were the losers. We missed them to begin with, when their experience could have been valuable for all the team but particularly for the younger players who were coming in. But, in the end, they missed out on some of the successes they might have been able to share in. Or might have helped bring to the club a year or two earlier.

Apart from the travel problem there were a couple of bad apples in the playing squad which I inherited and I had to get rid of them. It's only when you stop playing that you can look at players and spot potential troublemakers. We have been fairly lucky in my years as manager here. We have always tried to take a long, hard look at a player's character before going in and signing him. I don't think there is anything worse than having someone in the dressing-room who will cause unrest. You don't need that. I certainly don't need it. I have enough problems with the players because of the demands I make on them without having to worry about their behaviour!

If there are certain aspects of a player's life which are not 100 per cent right then his play will be affected. Drink has always been a problem with footballers and it's one that I have difficulty understanding because I've been a teetotaller all my life. People who saw me on television joking about taking a sip of champagne out of the League Cup after we had won it maybe didn't realise I was serious when I said that I hoped my mother wasn't watching. We had a strict family upbringing. My mother and father were Gospel Hall people and that's how we were all brought up. I don't take a drink and I have never taken a drink. Growing up in Ashgill, in the family environment we had there, moulded a lot of my character, I suppose. Certainly it meant that I wasn't going to be a drinker.

I think my family background also helped in other ways. My parents never wanted us to "bite off more than we could chew". When my youngest brother Tommy was turning senior, Scot Symon of Rangers came to the house and so did Willie Waddell of Kilmarnock. My father advised Tommy to go to Kilmarnock rather than join Rangers who were the biggest club in the country at that time. Tommy listened and had tremendous times with Killie before eventually being sold to Rangers when Willie Waddell had gone there to be the Ibrox manager. It worked out right for Tommy and I think his upbringing helped keep

Another manager who worked miracles at an unfashionable club — Notts Forest's Brian Clough. Here he is with Jim McLean at Tannadice before the two clubs played a friendly game. (Courtesy of D.C. Thomson.)

his feet on the ground. The realistic way we all look at things comes directly from the family.

I have needed all that realism in my career and especially since becoming a manager. It's only realism that helps you get through the difficult times which hit every small club. Without a strong, healthy dash of that you would soon find yourself in real trouble trying to deal with the various situations which can crop up. It also helps focus your mind on the financial worries which can afflict a club such as Dundee United.

The knowledge that you must scrimp and save and look after every penny has governed a lot of my thinking. Even now with the club financially strong I still stick to the early principles because I cannot abandon them. In a sense it has affected the team when we go into big games. You can never get away from the fact that you are a provincial club. When we walk into Ibrox, for example, you know you are going to play a powerful team, a top team. OK, we are one of the top teams in the Premier League set-up too. But we cannot match them for wealth and power and so we feel like second-class citizens when we walk in the front door and all too often when we have gone there we have carried that inferiority complex out on to the field with us. That has hurt me — but I don't honestly know how I can change it. When you are at a small club cutting expenses wherever and whenever you can it's difficult to be able to tell players that they shouldn't feel inferior to other teams who are so obviously bigger and more powerful than we are. You can't ban players from the snooker table at Tannadice because the cloth has been ripped and then instil in them some kind of arrogance or confidence or self-belief that arrives naturally at the bigger clubs.

This kind of pressure has meant my spending too much time on the parts of the job I don't like. The administration has had me bogged down too long and too often recently and that is why, I suppose, I can see myself leaving the job soon. You can talk all you want about the pressure which goes with big jobs but the real pressure is in staying in one job with a relatively small club and trying to maintain certain standards there. Ask Brian Clough, for example, how hard it has been for him to remain successful with Notts Forest. He has only to drop a little below the very high standards he has set himself and people start talking about him as a failure. Like myself, Clough could have walked out on Forest and gone into another job. A top job. That would have eased the pressure on him. I remember Jock Stein talking to me after we had won the Premier League Championship. "What more can you

MY LOVE AFFAIR WITH DUNDEE UNITED

The beginning of a long and successful partnership as Jim McLean joins Dundee United as team manager. Outgoing boss Jerry Kerr shakes hands with the new man while Chairman Johnstone Grant looks on. Grant, says McLean, was like a father to him. (Courtesy of D.C. Thomson.)

do for this club?" he asked. He was right to a large extent. Winning that title was the high point as far as success was concerned and to repeat that would be a miracle for us. The expectations grow within the club itself and also among the fans. I said earlier that the supporters now expect us to be in Europe but they also expect us to be in cup finals and in semi-finals and challenging for the championship season after season. This is what builds pressure on a manager.

I know that I still demand too much from myself. It would be nice if I could be a more relaxed kind of person — but it's too late to change. I still have this obsession for the game and until I get out of football I won't be able to alter that no matter how much I try.

The one thing I have done, though, is stay away from the dugout as much as possible. I will never go back into that dugout permanently. If I did I would be killing myself. I'm not saying that lightly. The death of Jock Stein in the dugout at Ninian Park in Cardiff towards the end of the World Cup game with Wales made all of us sit down and take stock of ourselves. Before that tragedy I had felt that I was damaging my health by sitting there. I saw what happened to Jock happening to me. It's a terrible thought and even though I have tried to take the lesson to heart I still find it difficult to do so. Even by staying away from the dugout I cannot help myself from getting very emotionally involved in every game we play. I worry about that constantly. But even if the public think that I'm cheating them by not going down into the dugout at every game I won't go. I'm not prepared to give all that I gave in the past. I think as you get older you have to change. You must try to adapt and that's what I have been trying to do. But it's not easy for me because it is so much out of character.

We were in tatters when Walter left this club. Losing him wasn't just losing an assistant. We had a unique relationship, a very special understanding and a deep mutual respect for each other. It was incredible how well we worked together. It was like I had been when I started out as a coach at Dundee and John Prentice was manager. Just as Prentice and I thought alike on the game, so Walter Smith and I were on the same wavelength. He was never a great player but you could sense in him that he had the ability to become a good coach. He was one of the players in the dressing room who was always ready to ask questions, always wanting to learn.

I can remember once he sat there in the dressing room and began to tell me what Sir Alf Ramsey had been saying about some aspect of the game. I blew up and told him — "Never mind what Alf Ramsay says — just remember you're playing for me." But he had been reading about the game, trying to pick up more knowledge about the game and that showed all the time.

It was important that he asked these questions too. Sometimes players sit there and just listen. They never query anything and you are left with the impression that they are agreeing with everything that you say. Often that's not the case at all and later it can lead to conflicts. So when someone is ready to stand up and argue or question or make a point then you know that they are thinking about the game. Probably that's why I chose Walter Smith to be my coach here. There might have been other reasons, I don't know. I honestly don't — but I do know that the choice was the right one for me. And for this club. He was Dundee United through and through. A magnificent servant for the club. Losing him was unbelievable. It could have brought a complete breakdown of all that we had been building here, and all that we were still trying to achieve. Losing him was worse than losing any player. It was a big blow to this club.

I saw this happening three years or so ago because it was obvious that someone would come for Walter Smith. He was outstanding as a coach and he has all the attributes that a top-class manager needs. Anyhow, I brought Gordon Wallace on to the staff because I was scared that Walter would leave. Gordon came in and helped with individual coaching and then when Walter left he stepped in as my right-hand man and has done a tremendous job. But Walter and I were very close. And I like to think we still are. You know, in all the time he was here he never once asked for a rise. In fact, I can't remember him asking for anything! He just did his job and any success he gets now will really please me. He deserves to be successful.

His departure meant that the season we went to the UEFA Cup final was a particularly difficult one for the club. The whole place was shaken to its foundations and that's probably why doing so well in Europe gave me an extra kick. We managed to do that against all the odds really. But even that run hasn't changed my mind about quitting the job soon. I'm looking forward now to the day I can finish. Inside the next couple of years I'll spend my time relaxing on the golf course instead of crucifying myself at games week after week.

I don't feel as driven as I was in the earlier years. Possibly I feel now that I have realised my full potential as a manager and perhaps, also, Dundee United has realised its full potential as a club. The club is as solid and respected now as it will ever be. Solid on the field because we still have good, quality players. Solid off the field because we have close to a million pounds in the bank!

I honestly believe that the club has gone as high as it can ever go and that very soon now someone else should be given the manager's job and then be left to get on with it. Perhaps they would be able to get more out of the players than I can nowadays. Perhaps the change at the top would help revitalise the club because I don't think I will ever be able to give as much of myself to the job as I have done in the past.

A year after I'm out of the job — or maybe even a month — I might well change my mind. But I don't think so. For 16 years I have known nothing but hard, almost unremitting, work because the manager's job at a small club like this one is very, very difficult. You are constantly being crucified by what I call the "bank balance chair" — the one where you have to sit down and take a long, close look at the finances of the club. Every decision you make is governed by what you decide in that chair.

It's hard to remain loyal to a small, relatively unfashionable club. I reckon it would be much easier to be loyal to a big club with a strong tradition and a massive support. There are many, many clubs which are bigger and better than Dundee United. But I will never ever have the feeling for another club which would match how I feel about this one. Probably Billy McNeill has that kind of feeling for Celtic. I saw that he said he felt that he was "back home" when he returned to take over at Parkhead again. I knew exactly what he meant. It sums up very well the way I feel about Dundee United. There were the good times at other clubs which I can recall but nothing compares to the family feeling there has been here. The club and the players, the directors and even the ground itself is in my blood now. I would never want to work anywhere else.

When I do quit I want to see the club continue being successful and I want to be able to leave a strong playing staff for whoever comes in to take on the job. It will be a difficult job for anyone to take on. I know that. The reasonable amount of success that I have enjoyed ensures that a new man in the job will have to live, for a little while at any rate, in my shadow. That's why I would like to be able to leave good players and young players and players who will continue helping the club be successful. We have Paul Hegarty and Dave Narey and Paul Sturrock now on the wrong side of 30. But we also have a nucleus of younger players within the club. For example there is a strong group of players who are under 25 years of age — a couple of them international players like Maurice Malpas and Jim McInally. There are also Iain Ferguson, Kevin Gallacher, Dave Bowman, John Clark, Harry Curran and our new signing from the Highland League, Hamish French, who come into that category. Just as important, our youth policy is still producing players and a whole group of teenagers are also on the staff. That is a stark contrast to the two "S" form boys I inherited when I took on the job.

Personally, I believe that a manager who is leaving a club must have some kind of legacy on the playing side to hand on to his successor. Because if that doesn't happen then it's on the cards that the man

The house that Jim built — or rather one of the houses built by United manager Jim Mclean. Here his wife Doris is seen standing outside the house where the family live now.

coming in will get the sack. So I would want to leave a good squad, leave something for him to build on, something which would make any other manager want to take on the job.

The one thing which hurts me about the present squad is the number of buys it contains. I may be a million pounds ahead on transfer deals but I'm still ashamed that the squad has six or seven buys in it. I always prefer discovering young players and then bringing them through from youth teams into the reserves and then finally into the first team. That gives me more satisfaction than anything else. Initially I didn't like asking the directors for any money to buy players and so I spent my time wheeling and dealing in the transfer market — selling someone and then using that money to get in another player or players I wanted. But even doing that didn't suit me. Buying a player is no substitute for finding a youngster and seeing him grow up and develop his skills. That makes it all worth while. It's also what I see as being the manager's main job — rearing your own players. For a long, long time, I scarcely had any choice in the matter. We couldn't afford to do anything else. But even now that we can I still take more satisfaction from grooming players here at Tannadice.

Players such as Richard Gough, who had been turned down by other clubs and then made it to the World Cup with Scotland — mainly because of what he had learned about the game here with Dundee United, are great examples. Richard's rise in the game was gratifying for everyone connected with this club. It's an honour for the club to have a player capped for his country — but even more of an honour when the system used by the club has pushed him on to football's biggest stage. You feel a deep sense of pride when that happens.

We have seen it happen here a lot of times in recent years, which makes it hard to believe that not a single Dundee United player had won a full cap for Scotland until 1977 when Dave Narey came on in a game against Sweden as a substitute. Before then there had been Scottish League caps but no one had played in a full international. That appearance was followed by caps for more and more of our players. Paul Sturrock, Paul Hegarty, Maurice Malpas, Richard Gough, Davie Dodds — all of them home-bred players — joined Dave Narey, while Eamonn Bannon and Jim McInally have also been honoured. For a provincial club it is always something of an achievement when you have players selected for international appearances. It was even more of an honour when Alex Ferguson chose five of our players to go to Mexico for the 1986 World Cup finals.

MY LOVE AFFAIR WITH DUNDEE UNITED

Jim McLean, in the centre of the picture, scores for Dundee at Dens Park in a clash with Hibs during his unhappy playing days with the other Dundee team.

Gough, Malpas, Narey, Bannon, and Sturrock were all selected — and the first four players all took part in the match against West Germany. That was a magnificent honour for Dundee United as a club. I think it showed the respect that our players are held in and underlines, perhaps, the professionalism that has been so important in the growth of the club.

Chapter 10

TROPHY WINS AND HAMPDEN HEARTBREAKS

I have talked about the fact that the club had never had any international players until the late 1970s in the previous chapter, but they had not been able to win a major trophy in their history either, until two years after that first cap had been awarded to Dave Narey. Since being founded away back in 1909 as Dundee Hibs, the club had always played second fiddle in the city to Dundee. It was 14 years after that when the club changed its name to Dundee United but 70 long years before one of Scotland's major trophies was to sit in the Tannadice boardroom.

That first ever win, the League Cup in season 1979-80, still holds a special niche in my memory. Winning the Premier League Championship was a much greater achievement — simply because winning the title is always the main target for every manager and every team and every player. It is the tangible sign that tells the world that you have been the best team in the country over the whole season. But I can still recall standing in the board room at Tannadice a few hours after winning the League Cup and Ernie Robertson, who had had a long, long connection with the club was standing in front of the drinks cabinet with tears in his eyes. He told me then: "I never thought I would see this day here. I never thought I would see this club winning one of the major honours."

He had been an important figure in the club and when he told me that after our victory over Aberdeen at Dens Park I realised just what we had managed to achieve. It was something that generations of Dundee United supporters in the city had dreamed of. But, probably, like Mr Robertson, they had never quite believed that they would see these dreams come true. Why should they have expected it? All along they had been looked on as the poor relations in the city — despite the fact that all of us were doing our best to alter that. Winning a major trophy helped, even though the victory could not be at Hampden. The first match had been there, but after we had drawn with Aberdeen, the replay was fixed for Dens Park — the ground which had held all these unhappy memories for me as a player!

Aberdeen were formidable opposition, possibly even more formidable than either of the members of the Old Firm at that time. Certainly, on the way to the final of the tournament the team, guided by Fergie, had beaten both Rangers and Celtic. We had had an easier route to Hampden. We had met Airdrie in the first round and lost 2-1 in the first leg at Broomfield before winning the Tannadice return 2-0. Then, against Queens Park we managed to win both matches, including a rare victory at Hampden when we won there by 3-0. The next round saw us against Raith Rovers when we could only manage a draw at home 0-0 before scraping through by a header from Paul Hegarty at Stark's Park. Our luck in the draw continued when we were pulled out of the hat against Hamilton, my first ever senior team. That semi-final was played at East End Park and we won by 6-2 to crash through to the final of the tournament for the first time in the club's history.

We knew that Aberdeen, who were to go on to take the title that season, would provide us with a tough test, the toughest around in that season. We had already played them in the Premier League and lost 3-1 to them on our own ground. If we needed any warning then that was surely enough. We went into that final as the underdogs and for long spells in the game that was the way we played. Hampden, as I'll go into in more detail later, has that effect on our players!

The team I put out that afternoon at Hampden was McAlpine, Stark, Kopel, Phillip, Hegarty, Narey, Bannon, Sturrock, Pettigrew, Holt, Payne. It was not good enough to win in the end but it was good enough to earn us another try at the trophy when the game still finished level at 0-0 after extra time. So it was on to a midweek replay at Dens Park, a venue which suited both teams. Neither of us wanted to force our fans to travel and we were convinced that playing the game at a neutral venue which would be more easily accessible for the supporters would benefit the attendance. We were proved right because at Hampden the game attracted 27,173 while in midweek at Dens we pulled in 28,933. I changed the team a little for that replay — George Fleming took over from Iain Phillip and Billy Kirkwood was used in place of Graeme Payne.

We went into that game with more confidence than we had shown at Hampden and an early goal from Willie Pettigrew might have had a great deal to do with that. He scored the first goal after only quarter of an hour and I knew then, I think, that we were on the way to that first so elusive trophy win. Pettigrew scored the second goal after half time and then Paul Sturrock made the win completely convincing with a third goal before the end. It was a decisive win for us against the team who were to take the title and while we were to go out of the Scottish Cup early against Rangers and drop back to fourth place in the League it was a season to remember for all of us.

It's difficult to describe now exactly how I felt at that time. I was so pleased for the directors, for Ernie Robertson, Johnstone Grant, George Fox and Jimmy Littlejohn because I knew how much it meant to them. They all told me in their own way what it meant that Dundee United should at last win a trophy in their time as directors. I felt so pleased for the supporters. Many of them had waited a lifetime to see their team win some honour and I knew how they would feel. And I felt so pleased for the players who had worked so hard to get the success that night, and who had had to put up with the demands I had made on them.

Obviously I was happy personally because it was a vindication of the management methods I had been using and the policies I had been adopting since taking on the job eight years earlier. There is no magic wand which can be waved to build a successful football team. It had taken eight years of hard work to finally get a trophy into the Tannadice board room. There had been a big turnover in players in that time, a huge change in the running of the club and, at last there was a real and solid and substantial payoff. As well as a history-making one!

But none of us wanted to stop and rest on our laurels after that . . . the first trophy gave us a hunger for more. We had become winners and we wanted to stay winners — and the next season we repeated our victory in the League Cup competition!

Again that victory came at Dens Park and suddenly the ground

TROPHY WINS AND HAMPDEN HEARTBREAKS

Dundee United manager Jim McLean with the Scottish League Cup — the first major trophy won by the little Tannadice team. (Courtesy of D.C. Thomson.)

which I had hated as a player was providing me with my best memories as a manager! Again we had gone through the tournament without meeting a Premier League team in the early rounds, but this time we were matched against Celtic in a two-legged semi-final. That was the most crucial test for us and we all knew it, particularly when we missed the chance to build a first-leg lead at Tannadice where we could only manage a 1-1 draw. Earlier we had beaten East Fife, Cowdenbeath and Clydebank without too much trouble but stuttered against Motherwell in the third round, needing extra time to settle that tie.

Celtic, like Aberdeen the season before, were to go on to win the championship. They were the most formidable opposition we could possibly have met in the semi-finals. But, because it was a two-legged affair, I felt that it would suit us better rather than having to face them at say, Hampden, where they would have the advantage of their huge support and the confidence of playing there and winning there so often. It was a second home to them.

As so often is the case in football, though, the result you perhaps anticipate just doesn't happen for you. That's how it was with Celtic when they came to Tannadice, got a draw which suited them and left us once more as underdogs in the return at Parkhead which was set for the following week. The Glasgow team were strong favourites but in a strange way we had always done reasonably well against them. Going to play at Parkhead never gave us the same problems as we had when we were going to Ibrox. That was one ground where we found it hard to get any kind of result over the years. While we seemed to be able to match Celtic — and we had some great games with them — Rangers had some kind of Indian sign on us. They might be playing badly but almost always they could get a result against us. It's a puzzle which I have not been able to solve no matter how hard I've looked at it. There is no reasonable explanation as to why you should be able to do well against one team but fail against another so often. There is just no answer.

Fortunately, then, it was Celtic who were our semi-final opponents that year and even at Celtic Park we knew that we would have a chance of victory. But none of us thought we would win so stunningly. Striker Willie Pettigrew whose two goals had helped win the trophy the year before sent us on our way to the second successive final with a goal after just three minutes' play. When Davie Dodds and then Paul Sturrock scored two more goals we were propelled into a final which was also to turn out a "derby" game against our city rivals, the team from across the street, Dundee.

So almost exactly a year after that win over Aberdeen we were back at Dens Park in an attempt to lift the League Cup for the second time. Again the Scottish League Management Committee had agreed to the game being played away from Hampden to suit the fans. Again it was at Dens Park and we were asked to cross the road for a match which had a 24,700 capacity after improvements at Dens had reduced the size of the ground from the year before.

This time, of course, we were the team who had been made favourites by the bookies. We were the team expected to win this city clash. It was an unusual position for us to be in. But with Dundee still in the First Division — they were to win promotion to the Premier League at the end of that season — everyone looked to us to win again. I felt uneasy about that. I have never been comfortable in a situation where so much is expected from us. It is probably because of the self doubts which afflict me so frequently, and which still hit me even though I feel deep down that I have proved myself a success as a manager. Davie Dodds, another of our local boys, was the only fresh face to come into the team from the previous year. The line-up which faced Dundee was McAlpine, Holt, Kopel, Phillip, Hegarty, Narey, Bannon, Payne, Pettigrew, Sturrock, Dodds. The substitutes were Billy Kirkwood and Derek Stark.

One time Rangers' manager Jock Wallace and Jim McLean pose together on the eve of the Skol League Cup final — this time it was Wallace who took the trophies back to Ibrox. (Courtesy of D.C. Thomson.)

It was almost predictable that there would be no easy beginning for us — "derby" games rarely throw up matches which are one-sided. You can get them on occasions but, in the main, these are games where the form book can be tossed aside. It was that factor which was gnawing away at me most of all as we prepared for the match. And even during the first half when we failed to dominate as we should have done the doubts still bit into my mind. Then a minute before the half-time whistle we got the break we needed to settle the players and myself. Paul Sturrock sent in a cross and David Dodds was there to finish it off with a header to give us a half-time lead and to leave Dundee pondering at half time on what might have been if the whistle had just gone those 60 seconds or so earlier. It would have been a pyschological boost for them if they could have held out until the interval. Instead we were the team who were lifted at half time. It's amazing how games can hinge on moments like that — confidence-boosting moments which can come at crucial times in a match.

In the second half Paul Sturrock scored another two goals, each of them following headers from Paul Hegarty which had left the Dundee defence in trouble. These were more than enough to give us the Cup for the second time and the pressure which had built on the club in the weeks leading up to the final eased considerably. Just a week before facing Dundee, for instance, we had crashed to a three-goal defeat from Celtic at Tannadice as they took revenge for their semi-final loss. It was hardly the way to get the team ready for the final, and particularly one loaded with the special worries and problems that only a "derby" match can provide.

It was funny, you know, in that season how we did against Celtic. We beat them in two semi-finals, because the League Cup win was followed later in the season by a Scottish Cup success — one of the few times we managed to record an important victory at Hampden. Yet in the League they were to beat us four times. That was anything but our normal form against the men from Parkhead — but even though any defeat hurts I was happy enough to swop these League losses for the two semi-final successes, particularly the first one which brought us our second trophy.

But while we had all the joys and the happiness of winning these two Cups the ultimate prize was the Championship. My views on the Premier League are in another chapter and so you know how difficult it is for any team to become champions in such a competitive atmosphere. That is why it is one of the most outstanding achievements of all for a club like Dundee United.

The other half of the New Firm, Aberdeen, had shown us what was possible when they took the title in 1980. Apart from the first season of the Premier League when we just escaped being relegated to the First Division we had not dropped out of the top five. We had been third twice; fourth three times; and fifth just once. The title, though, seemed to be beyond us, even though dreams had come true for the club and the supporters in the two League Cup wins. Even the following season we did get to the final again only to lose to Rangers. But it was the following year again that the title was won, and with that strange twist which football seems to produce so often our final game to clinch that championship took place at Dens Park. Once more it was at the ground of our greatest rivals that we were to land a major honour.

That Dens Park finale, of course, was only the last game out of a total of 36 matches played across the season. Unlike the League Cup — or indeed any Cup — there was no easy passage available to a team which aspired to be champions. We might have won our first trophy without meeting another Premier League side until Aberdeen in the final. We might have won the second and only been drawn once against another top ten team, Celtic, in the semi-final. But in the championship race itself you were asked to face the other members of the League four times each before you could be named as champions.

Our average attendance that season crept up to more than 11,000 people but that was well below the Old Firm standards, and below Aberdeen as well at that time. That is why it was such an outstanding success for the club. Yet there was a time just after New Year when I thought, and most of the country would have agreed with me, that any hopes of taking the title had vanished.

We had begun the season well and even despite losing heavily by 5-1 at Pittodrie, to Aberdeen — something which annoyed me intensely — we had reached the halfway stage with just one defeat registered against us, and we had lost only 11 goals — almost half of these in that Pittodrie trouncing! But Aberdeen beat us 3-0 at Tannadice on 3 January and that month proved disastrous for us. We lost to Rangers, could only draw with Hibs and although we beat St Mirren in a League game, we crashed out of the Scottish Cup in the first round proper at Paisley. When we went out of the UEFA Cup against Bohemians of Prague in the quarter-finals of that tournament it seemed to many that the season was over for us. Aberdeen were at the top of the League. Celtic were tucked in behind them and we were three points behind the leaders in third place. Now we had to play Alex Ferguson's team again, and while we had lost to the Czechs they had just seen off Bayern Munich in the quarter-final of the European Cup Winners Cup. It was then that the team showed so much of its character by going north to Pittodrie and winning 2-1 on the ground where we had lost five goals earlier that season.

But it was on the run in to the end of the season that our resilience really shone through. After we lost to Celtic at Parkhead they went to the top and were three points clear of us — and then came that last surge which took us to the title. We won our last six League games, including another visit to Celtic Park where we won 3-2. That put us just a single point behind Celtic. Just one week later Aberdeen beat Celtic, we won against Kilmarnock and for the first time that season we were the League leaders.

There were only three matches left. One of them was against Morton on a ground which had given us problems before and we decided at board level to help subsidise transport for the supporters who wanted to make the long journey down to Cappielow. They helped us win there by four goals, then that score was repeated at our home match against Motherwell and there we were with the finishing post in sight. Again that finishing line was at Dens Park where we had to face Dundee in the final game of the season. We won 2-1 with almost 30,000 people packed into the ground. With the win we clinched the title, equalled the points record for the Premier League and set up a new scoring record of 90 goals which we shared with Celtic who were in second place. They were just one point behind us and just one goal more had been scored against them. That is how tight the finish was. Aberdeen, our north-east rivals, were in third place on the same points as Celtic — 55. But if Fergie had to settle for third spot in the League he could console himself with the fact that his team won the Cup Winners Cup with a victory over Real Madrid in Gothenburg, and they proved themselves Cup experts by helping themselves to a Scottish Cup win as well.

The Scottish Cup, of course, remains the only trophy we have still to win at domestic level. I have managed to go with my team to Hampden four times since our first appearance in the final against Celtic in 1974 — and we have still to win the trophy. All of which, naturally, points up our failures at Hampden. These are underlined, I suppose, by the wins we have had in the League Cup, when both our victories happened at Dens Park.

So we have the Hampden hoodoo to contend with — and at our last appearance against St Mirren I found myself beginning to believe in it myself. Before the match I pooh-poohed the whole idea. Afterwards I wasn't nearly so certain because that is one final I had been confidently expecting to win. It was maybe the only time I had travelled to Glasgow for a final feeling relaxed and confident. On the other occasions we had had the Old Firm to face — never easy for a provincial side at Hampden. This time it was St Mirren, whose ground was a lot closer to Hampden but whose background was similar to our own.

The first victory in a major trophy and Jim McLean leaps from the dugout at Dens Park to salute the United players who had beaten Aberdeen in the final of the League Cup. (Courtesy of D.C. Thomson.)

We have played something like 13 times at Hampden and yet we have managed just two wins there. That hurts me. It also hurts me that we haven't been able to win a major trophy at the ground which is the home of Scottish football, the greatest stage the game has in the whole country. I would love to be able to say that we had won at Hampden. I'd love to be at that ground which has brought us so many disappointments over the years and finally manage to take the Scottish Cup back to Tannadice. But, now, I think any chance of that has gone. To some extent I've always gone into finals thinking that the chance would never repeat itself — this time I definitely believe that.

I don't want to take anything away from Alex Smith, the St Mirren manager, who is one of my friends in the game. I have a lot of time for him and a great deal of respect for him. It was some consolation to me eventually when I got down to realising that he had won the Cup after spending so many years in the lower divisions fighting to keep Stirling Albion going. If anyone deserved to get some little bit of success out of the game then it was Alex. But, to be blunt, that was the worst Scottish Cup final I had ever seen. I have been in some good finals with the team even though we have lost them all — but that game was a disgrace. An absolute, utter disgrace. I don't think that either of us deserved to win the trophy. I was ashamed that it turned into such a non-event. And I was ashamed that Dundee United did so little to help make the final as memorable as the others we have played in over the years. We did have a goal disallowed and that might have helped us win the Cup, but it's only hiding from the truth to make too much of that incident. OK, it was the second time a controversial offside decision has gone against us in a final at Hampden but, still, we simply didn't play well enough to win.

I contributed to the defeat myself because I boobed over the choice of substitutes. Initially I was set to leave out Paul Hegarty because he had been toiling after injury. My idea was to have Billy Kirkwood on the bench, mainly because he would have been a better choice as one of the substitutes in any case because he is more versatile. He can perform efficiently in several different positions. But I sat down and thought it over and when I remembered all the great things Paul Hegarty had done for the club and realised how disappointed he would be I changed my mind. That was a mistake — Kirkwood should have been on the bench. In some ways, though, it's a mistake I might make again, because in spite of the hard image I seem to have earned for myself I care for these players. I could easily do the same again if it involved one of the players who has stayed loyal to this club and who has contributed as much as Paul Hegarty has done in his career at Tannadice.

On that day at Hampden we could not get even close to our real form. Jim McInally, for example, who typifies so much of what I want to see in the club, couldn't raise a gallop. His legs had gone and that happened to other players too. The season had drained too much from too many and we paid for it with these two final defeats. Honestly, against St Mirren we had seven pathetic performances from players. We had four players playing towards their potential — and we need to have nine players reaching that stage if we are to win games, especially important games like Cup finals.

There was some criticism from inside the dressing-room about our preparation for the final. Not regarding the performances. Not looking at what had happened out on the field where things count most of all. But criticisms were aimed at the peripheral things, at some aspects of the build-up to Hampden. Yet nothing had changed. Not a single thing was altered as far as myself or any of the backroom staff were concerned. We headed towards that final in the same way as we had headed towards Barcelona or Moenchengladbach. The vital difference was the way the players dropped their level of performance during the match. At other times I've been criticised for moaning and groaning and demanding too much from players when it comes to Cup finals. I don't accept that view because I don't think it is true. If anything, I am more low key about a final because I see games as big as that as more or less self-motivating for the players. It's a whole lot harder to try to motivate a team on a miserable wet afternoon at Cappielow against Morton than it is at Hampden in a final. Without any shadow of doubt, I get on to them far less when it comes to finals. If players cannot lift themselves to extra heights when they can perhaps be earning thousands of pounds as a Cup-winning bonus, or cannot lift themselves when a Cup victory can give them some kind of immortality, then when can they do it? The pressure was on them without my adding to it. I would feel far more guilty today if I had added to that pressure which existed. I had to try to lessen that burden for them.

After a cup final is probably the time I say least to them. I can sense the disappointment that defeat in a final brings. I feel it myself and I know that the players will be feeling the same. What can you say then that would make any difference? A defeat in a final says everything, but against St Mirren it was probably worse because we believed that this was the one we would win at least. Before then our defeats had come twice from Celtic and once from Rangers in a replay. None of us genuinely thought that St Mirren would throw up the worries that playing either member of the Old Firm can do. But once again we sold ourselves short at Hampden. I'm now convinced in my own mind that the players believe that there is a hoodoo which strikes them at Hampden. They won't admit that if you ask them about it. They will deny it probably. But something goes wrong with the players when they play there in important games. Individual performances are affected badly and I would ask every player who has played for Dundee United in a Cup final at Hampden to look at themselves and then explain uncharacteristic displays. Or, even worse, uncharacteristic mistakes they have made in the games.

Take Hamish McAlpine and the two goals he lost against Celtic. Or the chip shot from Ian Redford when he was with Rangers which beat Hamish. Or there was Paul Hegarty heading five balls into dangerous situations in games. To Redford once, to John Colquhoun once and to Roy Aitken on another occasion I can remember and these errors have crucified us. Yet, the other side of the coin is that players such as Hamish McAlpine and Paul Hegarty were so often responsible for taking us to finals. They were marvellous servants to Dundee United in those years when we were reaching our peak as a team.

My own performance as a manager against St Mirren the last time we were at Hampden was disappointing too. The team selection was wrong, the players I took off were wrong and the timing of the substitutes was wrong. Kevin Gallacher should have been playing from the start.

All of the defeats have hurt, but probably none more than that one against St Mirren. I think that finally showed me that I'm just not going to win the Scottish Cup. The message got through to me this time. I suppose you always go into finals thinking that this will be your last chance. But I do believe that St Mirren was the last chance for me. I thought that when we played Celtic and we got another chance — and then blew it. I've never said to the players that this was the last chance, that there might never be another opportunity. I hope it won't be, but I fear deep down that it is. I don't see myself back at Hampden.

It hurts me that I haven't won anything at Hampden. It hurts me deeply, in fact. But being able to win the Cups and even clinch the League at Dens Park was some consolation for me personally. That made up for my troubled times as a player there and for my failures against them when I was a player. I was always able to get goals. I scored

The family McLean as Jim and his wife Doris relax in their garden at home with sons Gary, left and Colin standing behind them. (Courtesy of D.C. Thomson.)

on every park in senior football that I played on, but I never once managed to get a single goal against Dundee. So if Dundee gave me nightmares during my career as a player at least the ground brought me my best moments as a manager. Irreplaceable moments. Three games I will never forget and three games I can look back on with pride. Pride in the players, in the club and in myself.

Unlike those times at Hampden when we have had to travel back to Dundee still tasting the bitterness of defeat. But, even worse, having to acknowledge that we had let down ourselves and our supporters. That is the deepest hurt of all. And it's one which never heals.

Chapter 11

THE PLAYERS WHO MADE IT POSSIBLE

I think I said somewhere earlier in the book that a manager cannot turn a bad player into a good one and so if you don't have good players then you will fail as a team boss. It is just about as simple as that. Anyone, no matter how much of a miracle worker he may seem to be as a manager, must have good players to support him. In the years at Tannadice I have been no different from anyone else in that respect, and for the short time I intend to stay on in the job it won't alter any.

I don't believe in putting any of the players who have been at the club ahead of others because in a whole lot of ways that's impossible. Andy Gray was a magnificent player here, but there was no way in the short time he was at Tannadice that he could have made a bigger contribution to the club than long-time servants like Doug Smith, who is now a director at the club, or Hamish McAlpine who played for so long in goals. The outstanding thing about Andy Gray was that he was a born winner. It's a tragedy that injuries have cut down his chances of winning Scotland "caps" for instance. Yet I almost lost him. Sometimes, maybe all the time, there is an element of luck attached to signing young players. The first time I saw him he had a nightmare. He came up with four other laddies from Glasgow and he didn't look a player at all. My scout in the Glasgow area, Maurice Friel, had sent him and I had to say that Andy was terrible. But both Andy and the scout

JOUSTING WITH GIANTS

Two of the players who worked hard to make themselves better professionals — Paul Sturrock and Davie Dodds, now with Aberdeen, flank McLean in this picture at Tannadice.

asked for another chance and that's when I saw all the qualities that made Andy Gray a great player. He came up for that second trial and scored a goal with his head. I had him signed at half time during the game. I was frightened of letting him leave the ground. From then on, every time I saw him play he was scoring goals and almost all of them were headed. His aerial power was incredible.

He made me more than I made him. I didn't help him develop except in small ways but he made me more secure as a manager. I didn't have to do that for him as a player. He reeked confidence. Finding Andy

THE PLAYERS WHO MADE IT POSSIBLE

The Brothers — rival Premier League managers Tommy McLean of Motherwell and big brother Jim at Fir Park.

Gray made me start to believe in myself as a manager. He was just born a great player — and someone who wanted to win at all costs. He didn't like having to recognise defeat. If we had ever been lucky enough to

159

have Andy Gray and Richard Gough together in the same team then we would not have had our dismal record at Hampden. They would not have tolerated that. It would have been an insult to them. But we had different types, refined, nice, polite characters which is what I wanted in most ways. But in having them we lacked the really ruthless streak that these other two players had.

Dave Narey was an outstanding signing and has been an outstanding player for Dundee United. He was playing for a youth team called St Columbus and Gordon Wallace was helping them out by coaching the youngsters in the evenings. This team just seemed to keep on winning and so I asked Gordon about the players who were there. He mentioned Dave Narey and so I tried to pin him down about him. I asked, "Can he tackle?" Gordon answered, "When he feels like it he will tackle." I asked, "Can he run?" Gordon answered, "When he feels like it or when he really needs to he can run OK." I asked, "Is he good in the air?" Gordon answered, "It is not his strong point but if he has to win a ball in the air then he will do it."

Gordon was right on the button. Davie Narey turned out exactly as Gordon described him. I don't take any credit for the way he turned out. No one could. He was a naturally gifted player and I signed him solely on Gordon's recommendation. I never even saw him play. You have to know Dave Narey well to understand fully the conversation between Gordon Wallace and myself. It's just that he will push himself only when he has to. If he is running against the slowest man in the club in training then he will beat him by a yard or two. If he runs against one of the fastest men in the club then he will probably beat him by the same margin. He is incredible. He was born with that ability.

We picked up Raymond Stewart around the same time, and again I took a chance and signed him without seeing him play. Talk about luck coming into it! Our former player, Denis Gillespie, had seen him play and recommended him strongly. I signed him and so we had two players, Dave Narey and Raymond Stewart, who were to form the backbone of the team and yet both joined us without my having seen them play. They were two of our best players. Dave stayed on and helped the club to all the successes they had, while Raymond went to West Ham and with his transfer money he made it possible for us to improve the ground and buy Eamonn Bannon — quite a contribution in itself.

Paul Sturrock was different from the other players I've talked about or mentioned so far. He wasn't blessed with the natural gifts of some of

The one that got away — Richard Gough who moved to Spurs after agreeing a long term contract with Dundee United.

the others. He has had to work and work very hard for everything he has got from the game. Sturrock was smaller physically so he had to work that bit harder. He had to learn and re-learn the game two or three times in his career and alter things quite dramatically to take into account the problems strikers have had to face — probably more than any other players in any other positions. Both Walter Smith and Gordon Wallace spent hours on the training ground with him and did a tremendous job. But their work would have meant nothing unless Sturrock himself reacted to what was going on in the club. He did and that made him the player he is today.

Davie Dodds was the same. I used to give him a hard time because he was not a natural player, not a player who had been born with great skills. It's funny when I look back at Davie Dodds and think about him in training. He was gifted enough to respond to the coaching which was done at the club. When he went full-time he was the most receptive player in the club. Receptive to ideas, receptive to certain approaches to the game. Seeing how he developed and how he eventually won a Scottish "cap" gave me a great deal of pleasure. Both he and Paul Sturrock were to some extent manufactured players who grew out of the coaching and training we worked on at Tannadice. It was good to see them successful. And they were successful because of the way they responded to the coaching and the training.

Hamish McAlpine was the one player who was able to destroy single-handedly everything I have ever thought or believed about the game of football. I used to hammer him at goalkeeping training and every Saturday almost without fail he would throw a ball into the back of the net. I've always preached that if you want something out of the game, if you want to be good at anything, then you have to work hard at it. Hamish didn't. Sure, he trained hard. He probably did more running than any other goalkeeper in Scotland would do. But don't ask him to concentrate on goalkeeping. That was no use to him. He wouldn't do it. He didn't like it. If you did force him to do specialist goalkeeping work then he was murder. He made it so it wasn't worth your while setting up routines for him. What Hamish had was an eye. He was unbelievable and that eye made him a top goalkeeper with us for a long, long time, even though he kept proving me wrong by his attitude to specialised training.

If I had an outstanding failure then it was with Ralph Milne. He should have been playing in World Cups. He should have won a bundle of Scotland international honours. It was a tragedy that that boy was not

Manchester United boss Alex Ferguson — so long the other half of the New Firm which challenged the long held dominance of Rangers and Celtic in Scotland.

playing for his country all the time. He had tremendous talent — and I failed with him. He did not have the right attitude to the game and I could not instil that into him. If I had had more Milnes to deal with then I would have been out of a job. I see him as a failure for me personally.

Luckily, to outbalance Ralphie, I had Maurice Malpas who is a

JOUSTING WITH GIANTS

manager's dream. And I had Paul Hegarty and Narey and Sturrock and all the others who have helped this club. Helped put Dundee United on the map. I truly love every single one of them. They will be astounded when they read that — but I hope they understand the meaning of the word love. Because I love them all and that includes Ralph Milne and any of the other players I had trouble with. Basically I feel I have always tried to do my best as a manager to look after the players because I know that without them there is no success available to the club. Richard Gough, Davie Dodds, Ralph Milne — probably all of them will be critical of me. But deep down I know that I have done my best for all of them and remained loyal to all of them.

Loyalty was — and still is — a strong ingredient in the teams we have had and still have at Tannadice. I have never asked the players to play for me. Nor to play for the club. But I have asked them to play for each other. That has been vital and that's why Richard Gough's attitude when he demanded a transfer hurt me. I was disappointed in him. I felt let down by him. I had no crib about Davie Dodds leaving because he had given years of service to the club and had fulfilled his contract. But I thought that Richard Gough still owed Dundee United and his fellow players something. For his first few years in the team he was an ordinary professional being carried by the more experienced players round about him. They took him through his apprenticeship and he should have been staying on to repay the longer serving players for what they had done for him.

Richard Gough still had four years of a contract to run. If contracts mean anything then he should have been honouring that. He wanted more money. He wanted £50,000 from the club. What was to stop him coming in a month later if we had given him the money and pulling the same act again? Nothing! Absolutely nothing! He could have done that — maybe he would have done that. He had been given extra money in the summer, the same money as all the exceptional players in the club. Richard Gough was not worth more money than any of the other top players at Tannadice. I think Richard Gough did what was best for Richard Gough. But I had to think about this club and the players who were willing to remain loyal to the club and their team mates. Dundee United has never been run to suit one individual. That is not the way things are done at Tannadice. Nor will they ever be done that way as long as I am manager.

He got his wish and his transfer to Spurs but what he did not realise is that he would have been sold by the club before the end of his

Paul Hegarty in Premier League action against Rangers as he challenges three Ibrox players in this aeriel duel.

The German goal scorers — Iain Ferguson and Ian Redford with their wives after flying home from their UEFA Cup semi-final win over Borussia Moenchengladbach.

contract in any case. He was one of the prime players to sell. He thought that he had beaten the club. He didn't. All that brought him his transfer was the fee which was offered. When you are getting £750,000 for a defender, then you take it. Basically it is always easier to replace defenders, no matter how good they are. It was funny when the deal eventually went through. He travelled to London on the Sunday and was to have talks with Spurs and with Chelsea. I was so disappointed in his attitude by this time that I didn't even tell him to get ready to go to London. One of the directors did that. Yet before leaving for London on the Sunday he called me and asked me for advice on which offer he should accept. I could scarcely believe it. Such disappointments are all part of football management.